BLOODY POINT 1976

BLOODY POINT 1976

BRENT LEWIS

White Rubber Boot Publishing, Centreville, MD

White Rubber Boot Publishing
1012 Burrisville Road
Centreville, MD 21617

ISBN-13: 9780692423356
ISBN-10: 0692423354
Library of Congress Control Number: 2015905486
CreateSpace Independent Publishing Platform
North Charleston, South Carolina

Cover Design by Laura Ambler

ACKNOWLEDGEMENTS

Foremost thanks to my wife, Peggy.

Thanks to the members of the Working Writers Forum: Linda Fritz Bell, Bill Brashares, Mala Burt, Helen Delaney, Anne McNulty, Marcia Moore, and Gerald Sweeney. Your input and support throughout this process has been invaluable.

Special thanks to forum member and cover designer, Laura Ambler.

Thanks to Norma Coursey, Dickie Coursey, Mary Ann Hillier, Kenton Kilgore, Mark Lidinsky, Joseph B. Ross, Jr., Steve Saulsbury, Beth Schucker, Kelly Nash Sell,, and Jeff Straight, for reading various versions of this manuscript. Your feedback was always appreciated and was always given serious consideration.

Thanks to Suzi Peel for your encouragement and editing skills.

Thanks to all my friends and supporters, especially my running buddies.

Y'all know who you are.

The Bay Weekly Observer
July 1, 1976

The upcoming weekend will be an exciting one across Maryland's Eastern Shore, as we, along with the rest of our nation, honor America's 200th birthday. From Pocomoke City and Crisfield to Chesapeake City and Elkton, Eastern Shore citizens will celebrate with parades, picnics, and flag-raisings.

Here on the mid-shore, Bicentennial celebrations include a service at the grave of William Paca, one of the signers of the Declaration of Independence from Maryland, and a house tour co-sponsored by the Historical Society and the United Methodist Churches. On Sunday, the Fourth of July, the Lister Aldridge VFW Post hosts a crab feast, the Little Miss Chester River pageant, and the Lion's Club fireworks display.

Up with People, the enthusiastic group of young entertainers who "travel the world spreading their positive message through song" will perform at the high school on Saturday night. A great number of tickets are still available.

CHAPTER 1

"**D**on't touch it, dingle dick."

That was one of the first things Harris Bradnox ever said to Tooey Walter. Tooey had lived every minute of his twenty years among Chesapeake Bay watermen, so "Don't touch it, dingle dick" didn't seem like such an impolite way to begin a working relationship, much less a conversation.

Harris Bradnox was a big fish in a marshy little tidewater pond. Two hundred stumpy pounds dressed in cuffed olive khakis, a plain button-down shirt, and spotless work boots. Tooey figured he knew what everybody knew of Harris Bradnox. Despite his five-and-dime clothing, Harris Bradnox was rich. He owned lots of farmland and bought more every chance he got. He had a pretty wife, and a fresh Caddy or Lincoln every time you saw him, each new car painted dollar-bill green.

The Eldorado convertible parked in the driveway at Bloody Point Manor when Tooey arrived that evening wasn't green though. It was red and shining and its top was down. The white leather interior gleamed. Just walking past, Tooey whiffed new car.

A squall was building down the bay, off to the southwest. Tooey sensed the summer storm before he saw it. In about twenty minutes, there was a good chance this showroom cherry two-door was going to get drenched. Sudden downpours on the Chesapeake can perform dazzling violence from a distance; but wrong place wrong time? Change-your-life intense.

The house was one of those telescoping brick rectangles built on the waterfront a century after colonists first brokered real estate deals with natives who possessed no concept of real estate. English-bond construction and sturdy; these manor houses landmarked shorelines and stayed in families for generations. They were steam cookers in the summer. By Christmas, even the ghosts in the attic shivered from the draft.

Harris Bradnox worked from an office above a four-car detached garage with a set of steep steps running along the far exterior. Though some of the houses in the new subdivisions featured garages, most people Tooey knew owned a backyard shop filled with crab pots or engine parts; nothing that could be, with fairness, called a garage. Since all his family and neighbors drove used pickup trucks, garages weren't worth anybody's trouble. A garage was a sign of affluence. Tooey Walter was impressed.

Tooey tried to peek in the garage's casement windows as he went past, to see what inside might be worthier than the red Cadillac, but the glass was tinted. He knocked on the door at the top of the stairs, and when nobody answered on the second try, he cracked it open and stuck his head in. There was a chubby dachshund on a couch snoring and chasing dream rabbits. Fat drumsticks paddled air. Wearing a thin pink collar with a red, white, and blue bow, she never lifted her head.

"Mr. Bradnox?" Tooey said, stepping over the threshold.

From behind a door on the other side of the office came a deep, muffled response. "Yeah. Come on in. I'll be out in a minute."

Tooey took a look around without moving too far in. There were shelves full of books and framed duck stamp prints on the wall. The paneling was dark, the heavy wood furniture darker. The antique desk, covered in papers and files with a typewriter resting amidship, was the size of Tooey's bedroom.

The young waterman was admiring a vintage acoustic guitar on a wall hook when Harris Bradnox opened the door of the adjoining bathroom. Mr. Bradnox was still bouncing up and down on the balls of his feet, like he was shaking his jimmy a couple more times without reaching into his pants. Bradnox said, "Don't touch it, dingle dick."

"I, I wa-wasn't going to, Mr. Brad-"

"You play music, son?" Bradnox's tone was resonant, relaxed. Tooey could tell he was used to interrupting people.

"No, no sir. You?"

"Good." Bradnox said as he poured a few malted chocolate balls from a carton and offered one to Tooey. Tooey passed. "Waste of time. Christ-muh-kill-me, kid, last thing anybody needs is another fruitcake cock-hound running around on stage in mommy's make-up and a pair of apple sack leather pants." He shook his head and ate a malt ball.

"You don't p-play it?"

"I don't 'play' anything. I work for a living." Bradnox walked over and studied the guitar with Tooey. "In the Army, I'd lent this G.I. a few bucks and was holding his guitar as collateral. He thought he was Elvis – it's the same kind that hillbilly plays. I think the kid's mother or girlfriend gave it to him. He didn't hold up his side of the bargain, so the day I mustered out, his guitar did too." Bradnox grinned sideways at Tooey. "Reminds me of lost youth. I'm sentimental like that."

Bradnox sat at his mahogany flagship. As soon as his ass hit chair leather, the pudgy hotdog snapped awake. She scurried across the office dragging her belly over the shag carpet. She put her front paws on Bradnox's leg and he lifted her, rubbing behind her ears and whispering to her before she curled in his lap and went back to sleep. "Mabel's an old girl," Bradnox said to Tooey.

He seemed like he wanted Tooey to say something. Tooey said, "When you called you mentioned you might, you might have a job for me, Mr. Bradnox?"

Bradnox patted the dog's peanut-shaped noggin. "I've known your family a long time. Your father was ahead of me in school, and your Uncle Crutch a couple years behind." Looking away, Tooey could not have told you where, Bradnox pursed his lips and gave his head a half-shake. "I miss both those boys. The times we all had back then ... it's a shame how much this place has changed since we come up. Wasn't many years ago this place was a Garden of Eden."

Harris Bradnox was a real estate developer. Tooey Walter didn't know many people who said one thing while actively doing the opposite. Tooey said, "Crutch was a real, a real, he was a real good guy."

"Do anything for anybody. Give you the shirt off his back even if it wasn't his." Bradnox popped a chocolate ball into his mouth. "You crabbing?"

"Yes sir."

"How's it going?" Bradnox asked. "Catching anything?"

"Not bad I guess. S-some days better than others."

"What're you getting for them?"

"Thirty a bushel for number ones," Tooey said.

"Oystering this winter?"

"Pruh-probably. Might try the clam rig here in a bit."

"Um-hum," Bradnox muttered. "Still using your grandfather's boat?"

Tooey bristled. He ran his calloused hand through his uncombed hair. "I b-bought the *Miss Ruth* from him." Truth was, Tooey still owed his grandfather, the ancient mariner known as Moviestar Walter, a balance on the workboat. Tooey had not yet taken title.

Bradnox leaned forward like he was letting Tooey in on a secret. "Either way," he said, "you're setting yourself up for a long arduous go.

Working the water will soon be a thing of the past. For sure it'll never again be what it was back in Moviestar's day.

"This year, next year, ten years from now? What are you going to do when the bottom falls out of tonging oysters and running trotline for good? I hear you're a smart enough kid. You need to get off the water. After Hurricane Agnes, how many oysters you think are left north of the Bay Bridge?" Bradnox asked.

"Hardly none," Tooey answered.

"None. Not a living one anyway. A million empty boxes smothered in run-off." Bradnox leaned back. "Watch, ten years we won't have a packing house still in operation around here. I guess there'll always be some kind of market to sell to, but don't think that'll mean you're still in business. You'll break your back harder and harder for less and less return. The Chesapeake Bay seafood business is going to be a memory, boy. We fished her dead."

Bradnox folded his arms and said, looking all serious at Tooey, "A smart waterman today better be thinking what he's going to do tomorrow."

"You're pruh-probably right about that," Tooey answered.

Bradnox shot him an odd look and moved on. "I have something you can help me with, uh..." He clicked his fingers twice. "What is it they call you?"

"Tooey."

"My problem, Tooey, is my daughter. You know my baby girl, Delores."

Tooey had been afraid of Dee Bradnox since seventh grade. "Yes sir. I went to school with her."

"Well then, you also know she's always been a wild child," Bradnox said, "a mixed up little ball of trials and tribulation. A hurricane in a trailer park."

Tooey kept his mouth shut.

5

"Annette, her beautiful mama, and I have tried to keep her out of trouble all her life. Sometimes with loving indulgence, sometimes with a strong hand; mostly with cash. Last time she ran off, we figured we'd let her try to make it on her own. Cut her off. Let her see how challenging it is out there in the world."

"That… that seems like a good plan."

"Well, it wasn't. She's worse off than ever." Bradnox rummaged in the top drawer of his desk until he found what he was looking for, then tossed a Polaroid in Tooey's direction. The dog snored. "She's in Baltimore. Up there with the jigs, and the Jew mafia, and the degenerates. She's on the goddamn Block." His sigh sounded unhealthy. "Taking off her clothes," he said. "And who knows what else."

Tooey Walter had never been to The Block. He'd grown up hearing bits and pieces about the infamous red light district, but by high school all the stories told of The Block involved out of control crime and fast, ugly street turbulence. In his senior year a couple of Tooey's watermen buddies thought they'd check The Block out for themselves. They went back after graduation. Said it was bad the first time and worse the second. They planned on going back soon.

The Block's heyday was long past. Now it sounded like a place where anything could happen, none of it good. Throw in crazy-ass Dee Bradnox and Tooey was looking for a way out of the job offer that appeared to be coming his way. He picked the photo from off the office floor. In Dee's crooked smile, Tooey saw a faint hint of the girl he'd known.

"An acquaintance took it last winter after a Colts game," Bradnox said following a silence Tooey didn't know how to break. "Says he can't remember which bar he saw her in."

"Wh-why me, Mr. Bradnox?"

"Working on the water holds no prospects. I was friends with your father and uncle, rest their souls, and I'm fond of your grandparents.

I'm sure they worry. They been taking care of you a long time, and they aren't getting any younger, right or wrong?"

There was another long silence. Bradnox continued, "Dee's mother is losing her mind with worry. If she's not paying some con artist a fortune to tell her our future, she's sitting in that house over there gazing into the past. She's hooked on that genealogy baloney. I tell her, looking up a family tree won't get you nothing but a face full of monkey crap. Try to make her laugh, y'know." He stroked his dog. "But no matter where she's looking, she don't see any future for her baby. And there ain't nothing funny about that."

To Tooey, Harris Bradnox looked like a statue beginning to crack.

"I don't love much of nothing," Bradnox told Tooey. "I love my wife, my daughter, and this mutt. It's time to bring my daughter back home. Show me what kind of man you might be. Get this done, and in honor of your uncle and daddy, and your grandparents, I'll find a place for you. Get you off the water and making some real money." There was a depth of vulnerability when Harris Bradnox said, "All you have to do is bring Dee home."

"Mr. Bradnox, I...I don't know if I'm your guy. I mean... does she even want to come home? Dee can fight. How will, how am I even supposed to find her?"

Behind Bradnox's leather chair sat a huge black combination safe with intricate gold trim. Displayed above it was what Tooey recognized as an expensive collector's-edition, double-barrel 12-gauge shotgun. Tooey wondered whose collateral that had been. Bradnox swiveled and opened the safe's door without spinning any numbers on the dial. Tooey couldn't see what was inside but he imagined overstuffed money bags, piles of cash, and shiny things.

The older man said, "There's a girl named Amy works at Polish Jack's sausage stand on The Block. She should be able to tell you where to find Dee." He put five one-hundred-dollar bills on the desk. "This'll be easy. You'll be back in time to set off Fourth of July fireworks with Moviestar and your grandmother." He slid the cash toward Tooey. "I'll pay you the other half when you get home."

"I…"

"Get Dee back here," Bradnox said, "and we'll see about getting you some real opportunity."

⚓

Tooey walked back past the red convertible. The top was still down. The sky had gone slate grey with the storm's imminent arrival. "Screw 'em," Tooey thought. If he could take work he didn't want to do, the Bradnoxes could batten down their own hatches.

Turning left out of the estate's long oyster-shell drive, Tooey sailed north in his secondhand pick-up truck. He pushed Aerosmith's *Toys in the Attic* into the 8-track player. A blue El Camino blew by in the opposite direction. Tooey thought maybe he recognized the car, but wasn't sure. His mind was elsewhere.

CHAPTER 2

Tooey filled the six empty gas cans that were strapped into the bed of his pickup, topped off his truck's tank, paid his bill, and drove over to the store.

General stores were once the meeting places of the rural Eastern Shore. For several generations these businesses were where farmers and watermen gathered to gossip, talk politics, or tell tall tales; where hardscrabble families shopped for the bare essentials they could not produce themselves. General stores had replaced the colonial ordinaries and taverns as the center of Shore living and were mostly a thing of the past themselves. This store kept a sliver of the tradition alive.

This store, 'The' store, was an institution selling everything from ammunition to zippers. The shelves and lopsided wooden floors were a jumble of household and canned goods, hardware, clothing, crabbing and fishing supplies, hunting gear, rope, paint, kerosene lamps, garden seeds, patent medicines, packaged vanilla cookies, chocolate sodas, rock and rye whiskey, lottery tickets, and beer by the case or can. A look around might reveal treasures seemingly delivered by time machine. If a customer didn't see something they needed, they asked, and after a moment's consideration and a few minutes digging, the item would be unearthed. The cash register alone was a thousand years old. When it wouldn't work the family who owned the store made change out of a cookie tin they kept on a shelf next to the cigarettes.

The owners maintained a policy that customers could "Take what you want when you need it, and pay when you can." It was an outdated way to do business, but it worked. Three generations of respected store-keepers had made themselves a comfortable life at the store. Profiled in a Washington D.C. newspaper, the current proprietor was asked about their liberal payment practices. He told the reporter, "If I made them pay, they'd stop coming in."

The store would soon close for the evening. The youngest daughter, fourteen years old at most, manned the counter. She was always a real smartass. Tooey liked her.

"Where're the grownups?" Tooey teased. "You know what you're doing behind that counter?" The small black and white TV was turned up loud and the phone rang with shrill insistence.

"What've I got to know?" the girl said. "Somebody comes in and gets something I take their money or write it on the list. Eugene can't have more than a six-pack a night and if somebody wins the lottery they have to come back tomorrow while somebody else is here. You win the lottery?"

"Not really. You going to a-answer that phone?"

"Not really. What do you want, Tooey Walter?"

"I want to pay up," Tooey said. The girl grabbed the plastic index card box that held the credit tabs of every adult male within a ten-mile radius.

"All of it?"

"Yep. How much?"

"Thirty-eight dollars. Buy one of these mood rings for five dollars and we'll make it an even forty-three." She held out a box the size of a mother's day chocolate assortment with green felt lining containing maybe twenty rings of various sizes and styles. Tooey had resisted the fad, but he was rolling in dough. He tried on a pewter one and it fit.

"What's grey mean?"

She handed him change from a hundred dollar bill and slipped a five spot into her change purse. "It means you're a sucker."

Tooey Walter counted almost four hundred fifty dollars burning a hole in his pocket. It felt good. Bad thing was he still didn't want to go to Baltimore.

CHAPTER 3

Tooey's people always did their best thinking in taverns.

Old man Earl Calf had owned the Towed Inn ever since he was young man Earl Calf. Earl knew everything about everybody who ever walked through his doors. From the days of pointy-coned missile bras and beehive hairdos to hot pants and tube tops, Earl always hired rough and sexy barmaids to work the night shifts. Their attractiveness ratio tilted toward sexy-rough by midnight. Earl tended to the Towed's daytime drinkers. He came in at closing time to collect his kisses and cash.

Tooey's dad got himself killed leaving the Towed. Wesley Walter the first. Crossed the double line picking his nose in his rear view mirror and plowed headlong into a beer truck on an emergency run. Everybody knew that's what happened because the uninjured beer truck driver said so.

Uncle Crutch never made it through his introductory month in Vietnam.

The barroom was decked out in the colors of the American bicentennial. The blue reminded Tooey of the water and calmed him, but the white felt blank, like loss. Red threatened danger. There was nothing celebratory about any of it.

There was, however, celebration. A big weekend was approaching. The happy hour crew was out past their typical last call, while the hard-partiers were gearing up earlier than usual. A couple stools remained empty down at the far end of the bar, around the curve of the J, at a dead end against the wall. Most of the action was over near the pool tables. Tooey sat as far away as he could and still get waited on. Anybody out for fun, or even interaction, avoided these seats. Tooey wanted neither.

The women bartenders, a decade older than Tooey, were working the busy main section of the room. They never paid Tooey much attention, anyway. Earl was still on duty from his day shift, picking up the slack. Tooey was that slack.

"Ten ounce?" Earl never had much to say to Tooey either. There had been afternoons when there was nobody in the bar except the two of them, and Tooey would nurse his suds in silence while Earl sat at the other end of the bar and watched soap operas.

Long but not wide, the Towed Inn was a one-lane bowling alley back in the 1930s and '40s. Converted into a billiards hall, for decades everybody just called it the poolroom until Christmas 1974, when an upstart competitor opened with nickel beer every Thursday night and a clever neon light that blinked OAR HOUSE on and off.

Before the ensuing bar wars of 1975, when Earl Calf remodeled and gave out matchbooks with Towed Inn written in cartoon rope, the poolroom sold beer, no firewater or food, and seated only a handful of customers. There was no telephone. There were a few long-punished tables, scattered wobbly obstacles that were knocked over every time a squabble broke out. A quarter century's worth of graffiti was carved into the cheap paneling in the men's room.

The tavern's layout and jukebox—Freddie Fender played as Earl served Tooey's beer—was the same as ever, just like the dead cigarette

13

and stale lager stink. Almost everything else was changing. With a souvenir matchbook shoved under a leg or two, four of the old tables had passed a recent cut, but the bar was bigger now, with a new oak top shellacked to a dull plastic thickness. There was painted drywall in the john, and anyone caught defacing it was barred. Loud second-hand pinball machines had been placed beside the veteran, older-than-electricity shuffleboard table. Watermen's wives were starting to come in without their husbands. There was toaster-oven pizza.

At least there was still no phone. If anybody wanted you they had to physically come get you from the Towed Inn.

Tooey got the sense he and his generation missed out on something that used to be here. Except for the white collar guys on their way home from work and the drunken townie Eugene holding down a corner stool by the grace of gravity, everybody in the place seemed too young to be allowed in. A few were. The drinking age was eighteen.

A pool player waved to Tooey but no one came over to say hi.

Tooey took the picture of Dee Bradnox out of his pocket. This time he could see all the way past the image to the tiny towhead who won county fair beauty contests despite her shyness. Dee was smart in school, much smarter than Tooey. She blossomed early and dramatically and was tortured for it. By ninth grade she was smoking, raiding liquor cabinets, and rumored to be humping like a nympho banshee on Spanish fly. Tooey wasn't sure, but he thought Dee's first arrest came the summer before their junior year. She was the rare girl who didn't graduate. The Polaroid provided a glimpse of the child she'd been, but it was fleeting.

Under the disco queen makeup, Tooey recognized Dee's ornery golden brown eyes and the joker's gap between her two front teeth.

Her smile looked almost real.

Tooey glanced at his new mood ring. It had not changed color. If it had, all that would've told him was that he was the same sucker in a different mood.

A

Anyone who ever spent any time out on the water, down the county slips, or around the packing houses, had a strong chance of earning a nickname. Tooey knew people called Seaweed, Fishlips, and Hardcrab. Inland you could pick up a nickname working in the field or sitting in a duck blind, and most volunteer firemen were called something other than what their parents named them. The most fertile local family trees harvested a perennial bumper crop of nicknames.

There'd been a Muskrat George, a Parson Island Jon, and a Dick Ricky.

Teeny wasn't. Barrel Head was.

Turkey. Stringbean. Tater. Mater. Watermelon. Pickle. Pie. A whole meal working one oyster rock.

On the Eastern Shore, a nickname, even an unflattering one, could be a term of endearment, a sign of being included; a lifetime indicator that you belonged here.

Alvin Herbertson had been called Clacker since publication of his freshman yearbook. There's a picture in it of him running track, and hanging out below the yellow piping of his green gym shorts is clearly one of his testicles.

Clackers were popular toys at the time. Bola-like and dangerous in a million ways, they were of a simple design. Two glass or hard plastic balls hung from a string and if they didn't shatter in a kid's face, they could be banged together over and over again with an increasingly annoying rhythm.

Thus 'Clacker' Herbertson.

Clacker Herbertson lumbered into the Towed Inn. Growing up, Alvin was a good-natured bully. He always had a loud and hearty laugh, but wouldn't hesitate to push a smaller kid off the jungle gym or wallop someone without warning. In the years after he became Clacker, bullnecked and barrel-chested, he could be the most fun person at a keg party or the scariest. He and Tooey never had a problem. Clacker walked right over and took the last empty seat at the bar.

"What's happening, cap'n?" Clacker Herbertson spoke low and graveled, a baby bear's rumble.

"How you doing, Clack?"

"I'm doing all right. Still working with my old man and brother." Both were named Bennett Herbertson, and they were bricklayers. Clacker was their cheap labor. "They're a pain in my ass, but we been busy. Lot of houses going up."

"How's Fry?"

Fry was another of Clacker's brothers. Fry worked when he could find a boat captain desperate enough for help to hire a stupid and lazy deckhand.

"You know Fry. He's a screw-up. He's never going to leave Mama's house."

"You still there, too?"

"I got plans though. How about a beer, Earl?" Clacker shouted. "And get Tooey another."

"Thanks," said Tooey. "What plans you got?"

Clacker wrinkled his nose and blinked with a facial tic Tooey had forgotten. Tooey couldn't remember the last time the two of them talked.

"I've been saving up. This fall I'm going to start looking for an apartment." He took a long pull off his beer. "What about you? You got plans?"

"In the long run?"

"Yeah. Long run."

"Nope. Stay with my grandparents I guess. They're getting older. They're pruh-probably going to need me more. I'm buying the *Miss Ruth* and just working every day."

A sharp pain ran up Tooey's back. It'd been happening a lot. One night a few weeks ago, he couldn't get off his bedroom floor for hours. He hadn't mentioned a word of it to anyone. Dealing with muscle pain was part of his job.

"Sounds shitty," Clacker said. "Been getting any?"

"You?"

"All I can, buddy-boy." Clacker blinked hard and fast. "You know, Tooey, it's none of my business, but you look and sound more like a sad sack than ever. Soon as I walked in, I could tell you was in a funk. Like you need some excitement in your life."

This from a guy who lost his front tooth when a chain he was holding snapped. On one end of the chain was a broken down Monte Carlo. On the other end was a knot of teenage boys riding down the highway in the bed of a pick-up, holding onto the chain that came apart and whip-cracked Clacker Herbertson across the mouth. Sam Miller laughed so hard he fell out of the truck, busted his skull, and had to be rushed to the hospital. Real exciting stuff.

"I bet ol' Moviestar," Clacker said, "when he was our age, I bet he didn't sit around feeling all bummed out all the time." Clacker grinned at Tooey with that missing tooth and looked like a Saturday morning cartoon character. "I bet Moviestar was up for anything that come along his way."

Tooey had nothing left to say. He finished his second beer, told Clacker Herbertson he had to work early, and thanked him again. Tooey was going to go do what he always did. He was going to ask his grandfather what he should do.

Clacker took Tooey's unoffered hand in a death grip and shook way too hard. "See ya, Tooey," he said. "Don't forget to go get yourself some excitement."

CHAPTER 4

Two in the morning is really two at night. No matter what anybody calls it, when the world is creosote black outside it's nighttime. As usual, all three of them were out of bed and moving around, but no one said much. If they did it was in unnecessary whispers.

Tooey's grandparents' house was home to Tooey even before he lived with them. Before his mother left and his daddy died, the clapboard cottage was the one place he was well fed and went to bed knowing he'd sleep through the night.

The kitchen smelled of bacon and coffee and countless past baked goods. As it was every morning, there were cold biscuits, jelly, and apple butter on the table and twin brown paper lunch bags on the counter near the screened back door. Every day Tooey and his grandfather told Ruth that she didn't have to do this, didn't have to rise with them, didn't have to make them breakfast and lunch, but neither of them knew what they would do if she stopped.

They took turns kissing Ruth on the cheek, Moviestar first, then Tooey saying, "Love you, Ma." She smiled and told them to be safe.

Tooey and his grandfather climbed into the red and white pickup his grandparents bought used when Tooey got his license. Lights were on in a few of the houses they drove past. Each and every one home to the competition, far as Tooey and Moviestar were concerned.

The public landing was little more than a bulkhead and boat ramp. With no capacity to moor there, the workboats instead harbored out in the creek, tied to long, skinny wooden poles handdriven deep into the mucky bottom. Without a word, Tooey untied their backyard-built skiff from a bulkhead piling, paddled out to the *Miss Ruth*, secured the skiff, started the workboat, and putted back to shore where he loaded his grandfather, the cans of gas, and two plastic barrels full of line and bait. Moviestar put their lunches and a gallon jug of sun tea in the cabin while Tooey started filling the workboat's gas tank.

The *Miss Ruth* was part of the Walter's family. Moviestar bought her years ago from a highly regarded local builder. She was a 36-footer with a shallow draft and an Oldsmobile 455 V8 painted fire engine red.

A few months ago, it became obvious to everyone involved that both Moviestar Walter and his Kent Island tuck stern were getting too banged up to keep working every day. Though Moviestar wanted to give Tooey the boat, Tooey insisted on paying fair price, so he was still paying. After last oyster season, Tooey overhauled the *Miss Ruth* and was now taking his grandfather out with him whenever Moviestar felt up to it, which was almost every day.

It was three thirty at night and they were first out. As they motored east toward a sunrise that was still just an assumption, another set of headlights pulling into the landing were soon left behind in *Miss Ruth*'s wake.

"Sputtering a bit," Tooey's grandfather said. "You hear it?"

"Barely. You got good ears there, Pops." Tooey was a mediocre mechanic. It was the one crucial part of his job he had no real knack for.

"Needs new spark plugs, distributor maybe. I'll take care of that for you."

"Don't mess with it, Pops. I'll do it one day next week. After the holiday."

Moviestar said not another word. While his grandson steered with a 2x4 prop stick, the seasoned old salt stood port, breathed in the cool passing air, and grinned. His full, burlap-colored hair blew like a schoolboy's. The pride showing in his leathered features was evident even in the clinging darkness.

Tooey was a tenth generation Eastern Shoreman. The Walters were following an occupational tradition that had been their family's calling for as long as anybody knew. Each morning's work honored all the tongers, dredgers, netters, riggers, and potters that preceded them.

In those magical hours that bookended dawn, Moviestar Walter, like his father and grandfathers before him, had found his passion.

His grandson had not.

⅄

First lay is all about identifying that edge between shallow and deep.

Tooey dropped a scrapped crankshaft into the water. Attached to that anchor was a mile of rope and a five-foot chain for weight. A marker buoy of three empty plastic bleach bottles set the trotline's starting point.

Moviestar let the baited line out of the barrel with deft hands. In two-foot intervals along the main length were chunks of bull-lip tied to the end of drop lines. Sometimes the professional crabbers used eel, but bull-lip cost less. The amateurs, the chicken-neckers, they used expensive poultry as bait.

No matter how carefully the line is stored, it's not always easy to keep kinks and tangles from starting the day off badly. Moviestar never had any problems with the line, not even with his arthritis.

Tooey steered the boat. The line tautened as it sank. There was no need for the sounding pole. The Walters had been working the spot for days and knew precisely where they wanted to be.

At the end of the trotline Tooey dropped a second crankshaft anchor into Eastern Bay. Except for a searchlight beaming out five feet ahead of the *Miss Ruth*, there was nothing to see. Everything was done by sense of touch.

They went deeper on the second lay.

"What do you think, Sonny-boy?" Moviestar asked.

"Twelve bushels."

"I say thirteen."

Hanging a few feet from the washboard was a section of pipe supporting two vertical rollers, chocks guiding the baited trotline. At the beginning of the first lay Tooey pulled the line and ran it over the pipe. Moviestar piloted. He slowly moved the boat forward along the line. As the rope and bull-lip moved up and past, Tooey, armed with a deep wire dip net, caught every crab that had taken the bait and neared the surface.

They didn't get but a few on that initial swipe, but that never meant anything. The next run was much better.

Tooey got his rhythm going: Drop line barely visible even with a whale of a crab hanging on. Brisk, accurate plunge of the net, so smooth if the water were glass it wouldn't crack. Dip under. Snag the crab as it falls off. Catch two or three. Drop them into the basket Moviestar had placed in the perfect spot. Do it again and again and again. Tooey's long sleeve shirt kept the roller-flung nettles from stinging his arms. He'd met people who called these things jellyfish. Tooey thought that sounded plainly uninitiated.

At the end of each line, before starting the next run, Moviestar culled. Using a set of tongs, he stationed one basket for the fat number ones, another for number twos, and one for females. Trash crabs and anything even close to too small got tossed back into the water.

Between sortings, Tooey watched his grandfather steer their boat.

Except for his time as a soldier in Europe during World War 1, Moviestar Walter had lived on the Eastern Shore all his life, and had worked the water almost as long. His daddy was said to be the foremost oyster tonger who ever stood on a washboard. "My father raised me for this," Moviestar Walter would say, "and it's all I know how to do."

Moviestar had been a husky man in his prime. Now at seventy-six he was hunched and gaunt, but he was still strong, with broad shoulders and corded arms, and his hands were the fastest Tooey ever saw. Moviestar's skin was sun-worn, and his grey eyes were heavy, but his hair was thick and his smile gleamed. Women of every age and type still flirted with Moviestar Walter.

This man was a bay captain. He needed no electronic finder to catch rock and bluefish, and knew by heart where all the best oyster beds were from Crab Alley Lumps to Starvation Hill. He was a mechanic, welder, carpenter, weatherman, and astronomer. His favorite foods included fried eel, muskrat, and Ruth's "turkle" soup. As is the waterman tradition, Moviestar wore no watch, but always knew what time it was.

For luck, he carried a pouch of salt in his pocket everywhere he went.

"Hey, Pops," Tooey said, "did Ma tell you Harris Bradnox called?"

"Yessir." Moviestar's voice was some lost thing from the past, all prohibition-era Canadian whiskey poured over shellfish midden. Moviestar always told his grandson that his accent was a result of the Eastern Shore's generations of tight knit isolation, and wasn't much different than their ancestors and distant cousins on the other side of the Atlantic Ocean. Moviestar called oysters *arsters,* hogs *hoags,* and water *wooder.*

Tooey waited for his grandfather to ask more about Harris Bradnox but he knew he wouldn't.

"He wanted to talk to me about maybe coming to work for him."

"That right?"

"I don't know doing what," Tooey said. "He wasn't too specific. He knows I don't have much experience with anything. I guess he might have something he thinks I'd be good at and is willing to train me. Real estate maybe?"

Tooey caught jumbo jimmies, those dark and hefty male crabs, on his next seven dips. "Look at that'n," Moviestar said. "Fat as Buck Jones' pony."

Tooey went on, "Mr. Bradnox has got a job he wants me to do this weekend. You remember his daughter Delores? Went to school with me?"

Moviestar was all business. "That chock is catybiased," he said, pointing. It was off a smidgen. Tooey toed it into place before his grandfather answered the question. "I recall a sweet little girl," Moviestar said, "well mannered. Bright."

"I know you've heard some of the stories about her since."

Moviestar laughed. "I'm too grizzled for stories, cap'n. What they say about people's neither here nor there and the truth's usually a whole 'nother story. You know that."

Tooey was getting nowhere. Sometimes it was like pulling clam's teeth.

"Dee's on The Block," Tooey said. "Mr. Bradnox wants me to drive to Bal-, to Baltimore tonight and bring her home."

"That don't sound too hard. Don't sound like a full time job, but don't sound too hard," Moviestar said.

"Mr. Bradnox doesn't even clear-cut know where she's at. Somewhere on The Block, he said. I'm not sure she knows I'm coming to get her or even if she wants to come home."

"Seems if she wanted to she'd have made it easier."

"I don't know anything about the city, Pops. What am I going to do if I can't find her right off? Live there until I do? I don't even know what else Bradnox has in mind for me. Maybe it's something I'll hate. Or something I'd enjoy, but if I blow this errand boy mission, I never get the chance. Never get the chance," Tooey mumbled without thought, "to get off this *god*-damn water."

Moviestar said nothing. Tooey's face reddened.

"P-plus I don't trust Mr. Bradnox much," Tooey said.

They worked in silence.

⅄

The sun rose hard at a quarter to six and the breeze dropped out. As they started their fourth run, the distant inland greens and gold of summer reminded Tooey of the cold winter months of oystering that lay ahead. Compared to hand-tonging for oysters, crabbing was easy work, fun too, despite the repetitious "baiting up, getting up, and taking up." Anybody who said oystering was fun should be avoided like a pirate with rabies. Only a maniac would enjoy standing all day above dangerous icy water with snot freezing on his face, raking the bottom with a thirty-foot pair of tongs fitted with heavy and pointy-toothed iron heads. Over and over, dropping those tongs into the water and hand over hand, all back-breaking day long, pulling them up to the boat, hopefully full of clean marketable oysters. What sort of nut could love that life, Tooey asked himself.

Nuts like Tooey's grandfather.

It was man's work. It was outdoors, time-tested, and in good years profitable. No other man was a waterman's boss. Mother Nature and, more and more lately, Maryland's Department of Natural Resources alone dictated the rules.

To Tooey, men like Moviestar were anchors forged of iron. They were durable and stable, providing safety and optimism that if you didn't over-plan, things usually went as planned. But those men were inflexible. This was the existence they knew. Tooey thought of the waterman's life as a rope tethering him to who he was, yet holding him captive by the very act.

After eleven runs in, they took a break to eat and talk with other crabbers on the marine band radio, all of them lying about their catch. Tooey knew to always judge a waterman's success by the opposite of what he says.

Moviestar smoked his one cigarette of the day while Tooey finished the second sandwich his grandmother always packed him. Tooey's back was aching.

His grandfather said, "I didn't know you wasn't happy out here, bunk."

"It's not that, Pops. I like doing this with you. But I don't know it's what I want to do the rest of my life. Way things are these days, even you have to admit it ain't easy."

"Nobody ever said it would be." Moviestar's feelings were hurt. Now Tooey was certain.

"This is all I've ever done," said Tooey. "Even if it's in my blood, and even if I come running back because I can't or don't really want to do anything else, I think I have to try something. I'm two years out of high school and feel like I'm a hundred years old."

"I know that feeling."

"Should I give Bradnox a try? I don't think I like him."

"Why you?"

"Said he heard I was smart."

"You are capable of anything you set your mind to."

"He said he was fond of you and Ma."

"News to me. I haven't seen Harris Bradnox to talk to him in a coon's age." Moviestar puffed his non-filter to a nub, and plucked it overboard. "Huh. Guess men like Harris say a lot of things."

"What do you think of him?" Tooey asked.

"I don't have particular feelings either ways. His parents are good folks. Known them all my life. Harris, I believe, might have a chip on his shoulder, something to prove. He's always been flashy and quick to spend good will on a hasty buck, though a lot of businessmen can be that way." Moviestar slapped his grandson on the knee. "But honey, if you want to be a businessman, you'll be the most honest, least chinchy businessman ever went into business."

"He probably wants to hire me to unload manure on one of his farms."

"Tooey, way you tell it, sounds to me Harris wants somebody he can trust to return his baby to him. It's a foot in the door with a man who carries a lot of influence. If you don't want to work the river all your life and end up stoved up like me, you have to start making decisions on which direction you're going to go. Durn, even if he don't offer you a full time position making thousands of dollars, maybe he'll do you a good turn in the future... On the other hand, you got to go with what *you* think."

⚓

While they were taking in their lines, Tooey asked, "What about you? What would you do?"

"Boy, you know I ain't rigged quite right." Moviestar stood as straight as possible and made sure Tooey was listening. "But no matter what you think of Harris Bradnox, he loves his daughter. People love their children. They protect them and want better for them than they had themselves. Much as it hurts, truth is there ain't much in it for you if you stay out here on the water. And you can't never change nothing if you're scared to."

Tooey smiled at the old man. "Plus I already took his money."

27

Moviestar chuckled and shook his head. "If you don't want to do it, I've got whatever you need to take directly down to him this afternoon and give it back."

"I didn't say I spent the money. And where'd you get so much extra loot?"

"You keep giving me your money and I keep trying to give it back to you." Moviestar smiled. "Just keep in mind, in the end, if you decide to become a big wheel, every once in a while even little dogs will come out of nowhere and take a leak on you."

Eleven thirty and headed in to unload at the buyer's waterside packing house, Tooey piloted and Moviestar talked on the radio, saying, "Not too good. We're probably going to move on tomorrow."

At the dock, Moviestar took pleasure in the protocol and social rituals of getting paid while Tooey washed down the boat. Thirteen *booshels* just as Moviestar predicted. Not bad at all, but not like the crab potters were doing. That was big business. Twenty-four hours a day, seven days a week. Moviestar never wanted any part of it, the old man loved hard work but was never greedy for it, and Tooey sure as hell wasn't interested.

They took their cash minus the cost for a tub of salted bull-lip. On the return trip to the landing, a couple dragonflies buzzed and jousted with each other around Tooey's head.

It took an hour to re-bait the line, replacing and throwing overboard any of the thousand pieces of meat that had bloated and turned alabaster. Even a scrounging scavenger like the blue crab would only degrade himself so much for a bite to eat.

As he slid behind the wheel of his pickup, Tooey tried one last time to get a straight answer. "Should I go to Baltimore? Would you?"

"Son," Moviestar said, "you are too grown for me to make your decisions. What I would or wouldn't do don't mean a lick."

"You don't ever change," Tooey said. "You know that? You just say it different. I'm starting to wonder why I keep asking you stuff."

CHAPTER 5

After the Walter boy had left his office on Thursday evening, Harris Bradnox tried to run the numbers on his financial situation again, but he'd lost his taste for it. Concentration was impossible. He hadn't slept well in weeks. His stomach was killing him. You didn't have to be a doctor to know there was a bleeding pothole of an ulcer inside him. Harris couldn't stay out of the bathroom. It was getting embarrassing.

The *Bay Weekly Observer* was handy, so Harris lit a cigar and leafed through. He wasn't bullshitting the kid, look right there – COUNTY WATERMEN FACE DIM SHELLFISH OUTLOOK – Dermo, MSX, 25-60% oyster mortality. Crab harvest down. Bay grasses disappearing. Jesus, Harris thought, the whole food chain was breaking down.

There was a report about 328 building lots being approved on Prospect Bay. Harris wanted in on that deal but it hadn't worked out for him.

The paper reminded readers that a morbid anniversary was approaching. Last summer, a bunch of strung-out druggies driving through on their way to Ocean City gunned down a local state trooper. Happened right up the road. And not long before that those poor girls got murdered in Caroline County. People never used to lock their doors around here. They did now.

There was a shanty explosion at Kent Narrows. The shanties were rickety tinderboxes where packing-house pickers and shuckers lived. To Harris it was a wonder the whole damned place hadn't gone kerpow. The explosion had killed a couple colored boys.

Some teenage simpleton drowned jumping off Cox Creek Bridge.

A write-up on the Little League All-Stars game was in the paper, as was the schedule for the upcoming county fair, and, of course, a list of all the weekend's Bicentennial goings-on.

A Disney comedy was playing at the Avalon Theater. The drive-in was showing Yvette Mimieux in *Jackson County Jail* and some chop suey *Enter the Dragon* foolishness. Harris used to like going to the movies, but couldn't call to mind the last time he'd been.

Life in general was beginning to blur for Harris Bradnox. And the events of the last few days, from an unsatisfactory meeting with his accountant to the unexpected phone conversation with his daughter, hadn't helped much.

Harris stroked his temples and let the cigar burn out. He felt sick.

Was that thunder? He remembered his wife's car and walked to the window to see if it was still parked outside. It was, the top still down. Plump intermittent raindrops were falling on every expensive upgrade that Harris was sooner or later going to have to pay for.

He was getting ready to go raise hell until he saw the blue El Camino coming up the driveway.

CHAPTER 6

The rain poured. Clacker Herbertson secured the ragtop for Mr. Bradnox. He wiped down the seats and dashboard. No towel was provided, so Clacker dried himself with the same damp shammy cloth he'd used on the car.

Clacker rubbed his crew cut hair while he and Harris Bradnox talked about a pair of homes under construction in the new Beachside Estates subdivision, a parcel of land Clacker's father called the old Coleman farm. The houses were good-sized two stories, eighteen hundred square feet, plus or minus. Herbertson Masonry had completed the brickwork on both of them the week prior. A third was due to break ground on July fifth.

"Thanks again," Bradnox said, "for running those contracts to Salisbury last week."

Clacker always liked it when Mr. Bradnox hired him to do odd jobs. Unload construction deliveries, plow snow, whatever: Clacker was always ready. The afternoon drive a few days ago had been particularly satisfying.

It had been blistering hot and he was on the jobsite, humping block for his father and brother, who'd been pushing each other, and Clacker most of all, to get this foundation finished before quitting time. Even went so far as skipping lunch. But when the head honcho asked if he could "borrow their slave," they couldn't say no. They had to bite their lips. Bradnox gave Clacker gas money plus twenty bucks. The looks on both Bennett Herbertsons' faces, as their slave drove off while there was still work to be done, would have been payment plenty.

"Happy to help out, Mr. Bradnox. Anytime. You've got something for me?"

"I might. I know you're tough, I was in the poolroom the night you sent those Pierce boys home in the ambulance, but I might need more than just tough for this job. How smart are you, son?"

That sounded like a trick question to Clacker Herbertson.

"Pretty," he answered.

⅄

Clacker listened to Mr. Bradnox some more, and thinking he'd gotten it mostly straight in his head, said, "So Dee owes you money and you're sending Tooey Walter to get it."

"And bring her home. You know the Walter kid?" Bradnox handed Clacker a malted milk ball.

Clacker ate it, and said, "Sure."

"What do you think of him? He's got a stutter."

"Tooey's alright. Kinda weird. He stutters when he's nervous."

"Good looking kid. Resembles his mother's side. Looks able enough. Is he?"

"Never played sports or nothing, but Tooey ain't no wuss."

"He's got none of the charisma his Uncle Crutch had, that's for sure. He's more like that dim-witted daddy of his," Bradnox said. "It's like you want to like him, but can't quite bring yourself to do it."

"Tooey's been like that since he was little." Clacker was always reluctant to goad authority figures, but he was excited about Mr. Bradnox's assignment. He brought the conversation back around. "So again, you want me to…?"

"I don't know exactly where my rebellious princess of a daughter is, and I'm not sure Tooey can handle the trouble that might spring up while he's trying to find her. The Block's a dangerous place."

"I don't think Tooey's been in a scrap since grade school. I been in lots."

"I'm sure."

"So you want me to follow Tooey to Baltimore and make sure Dee gets back to Bloody Point no matter what."

"I do," said Bradnox, but without the certainty that tinged everything else that came out of his mouth. "I do. But what's most important is that you bring back what she owes me."

Clacker was flat broke and needed spending money. Bradnox bitched some, a formality of doing business Clacker suspected, but he did come off a couple fifties. Said he'd pay twice that for the job upon completion. The young man trusted Bradnox without reservation. Later Clacker would wonder why his employer hadn't just sent him alone to get Dee. But it didn't matter, because even if he'd thought of it sooner, Clacker would not have asked.

Clacker was almost out the door when Mr. Bradnox said, "Oh, hell, wait a minute, Herbertson. Hold on." He opened a desk drawer. "Here. Take this."

CHAPTER 7

Clacker saw Tooey Walter's truck parked in front of the Towed Inn, went inside, and bought his old schoolmate a beer. Nudged him. When Tooey left, Clacker tailed him like he thought Jim Rockford would, or Mannix maybe. Clacker always wanted to grow up to be a cop. Now he gave some thought as to whether private detective might be the better way to go. The PIs got the chicks and cars, but not the uniform or clout, so Clacker guessed it would probably be a wash.

His intention was to stay on Tooey all the way to Baltimore and back.

What Clacker Herbertson was proudest of, loved most in the world, was his '72 royal blue Chevy El Camino SS with the black stripe on the outside and the interior Armor All-ed almost to a mistake. He called her Blue Lightning.

Clacker kept Blue Lightning a good half mile behind Tooey all the way, and then backed her into Blink Benton's junkyard. He watched Tooey pull into his grandparents' driveway.

Sitting among Blink's wrecks and abandoned rust-heaps, Clacker made an oath his baby would never meet their pitiful fate. He also vowed he would use Mr. Bradnox's important mission to prove himself. Prove he wasn't like his brother Fry, or his brother Bennett, but more like their one-eyed but successful and independent brother Gilmore, the marina manager. Clacker swore that by next year he would move out of his parent's house and get his own place.

Either that or buy Eric Nash's '68 Dodge Super Bee.

Bring Blue Lightning home a Mopar stepsister.

Tooey's house lights went off. Bedtime. Clacker eased the seat back, and fell asleep. He knew crabbers were early risers. He forgot how early.

⚓

"Cheese-n-rice." Clacker Herbertson did not like to take the Lord's name in vain, so when he opened his eyes and saw Tooey already gone, he said "Cheese-n-rice" instead.

He drove to the public landing where a dozen watermen's pickup trucks were parked, including Tooey's.

Clacker knew he had time to kill.

He rode around and watched the sun rise, and then he cruised down to the county slips and Cabin Creek, but nobody was hanging out deciding to kick-start a drinking day instead of a working one. And it didn't take long for the radio to bug him. Clacker could listen to southern rock, and bands like the Eagles and The Doobie Brothers, but he could go days without music and never notice its absence. Disco, particularly disco at daybreak, made him want to beat somebody with a platform shoe.

Clacker stopped at the Roundhouse Restaurant where all the area carpenters, house painters, and masons started every day with cigarettes and trash talk along with their coffee, eggs, and scrapple. All except Clacker's father and brother. This time of year those two started six sharp. The Herbertsons never cared much for socializing.

He sat alone at the counter and recognized the gray-haired waitress as somebody's mom-mom. He said, "A bowl of cream of crab soup and an ear of sweet corn please."

"For breakfast?" She looked right at the hole in his smile. The corn came out of the kitchen smothered in butter and sprinkled with crab seasoning, and it smelled like summer. It was so good Clacker had a second ear for dessert. He smoked Marlboros and wondered if he had room for a Tastee Freeze milkshake.

He filled Blue Lightning with gas, and at 60 cents a gallon it cost him damn near ten bucks. When he finally allowed himself to look at his wristwatch he knew he still had hours to go before Tooey might head across the bay.

He was already bored out of his mind.

Ending up at the Towed Inn as Earl was opening, Clacker drank draft beer, played pinball, and watched game shows on TV. What eventually ran him out of there was realizing he'd been in a too-long, too-close, and one-sided conversation with Eugene, who smelled like he hadn't taken more than a whore's bath since the invention of drugstore cologne.

The post office was at the corner of County Landing Road and Main Street. Clacker bought a copy of the county's weekly newspaper from a metal box. Glancing through it while sitting in his car in the parking lot, he got sidetracked making a list in his head of the things that got on his nerves: 1. His father. 2. His brother Bennett. 3. Disco-anything. 4. Foreign food. 5. Stupid sports. Examples: tennis and golf. 6. Science Fiction 7. Crowds. 8. Whipped cream.

And Eugene. Definitely Eugene.

⋏

Tooey and his grandfather drove right past and never even looked Clacker's way. They were headed in the dead-end direction of home.

Clacker knew enough about the water business to know getting ashore wasn't the last of it. Tooey and Moviestar were sure to still have work to do because a waterman's crap was always breaking or needing maintenance. At the very least, Tooey would have to clean up. Probably take him an hour or more just to wash the crab stank off.

Ever since the beer he drank had settled, Clacker couldn't stop thinking of that Tastee Freeze chocolate shake no whipped cream.

He figured he could scoot up there, breeze the Freeze, and get back before Tooey Walter even got his dirty white rubber boots off.

It took Clacker fifteen minutes, no more than twenty, to make his milkshake run. When he got back, Tooey's truck was, once again, gone.

Chapter 8

Tooey took a quick but thorough shower, threw a change of clothes into his old high school gym bag, and took off. His grandmother was running errands. Moviestar was out in the shop, busy with his soft crab sloughing operation.

The William Preston Lane, Jr. Memorial Bridge, the Bay Bridge to everybody except the State of Maryland, was completed four years before Tooey was born. His father had worked on its construction as a paid-by-the-trip barge operator. From what Tooey had heard all his life, the bridge's opening changed everything on this part of the Eastern Shore. Just not as lickety-split as some folks had hoped or feared it would.

Moviestar taught Tooey that before the bridge, the two halves of Maryland always harbored shared interests but were worlds apart. The Western Shore—Washington, D.C., Baltimore, Annapolis—was the seat of every kind of power that expanded in every worrisome way. The Eastern Shore, made up of small towns, farmland, and tough waterman enclaves, was the state's breadbasket. Seafood basket, too. Except for an occasional advancement in work methods or standard of living, for generations The Sho' remained as unchanged as anyplace in America.

Until the bridge.

Tooey looked for the appropriate tape and chose Heart's *Dreamboat Annie*. Ann Wilson's voice was like going to church, and for Tooey, there was no one hotter, no Playboy Playmate, no television angel in a red bathing suit, than Ann's sister Nancy when she was wailing away on her guitar.

According to Moviestar, except for one ninety-degree turn, Ritchie Highway was a straight shot all the way to the Baltimore City line.

⅄

When Tooey was eleven, his grandmother had "lady problems", and saw doctors in the city. She was never sick in Tooey's presence though, never spent a day in the hospital. He remembered going with his grandparents for one of Ma's checkups. It was Christmastime. Moviestar stopped at Harundale Mall on their way home. Decked out for the holidays with a giant twinkling fir tree, elves, and live reindeer; carols playing over the public address system while the actual carolers were on break, Harundale Mall was as close to the North Pole as any real kid was ever going to get.

His grandparents let him choose where they ate lunch. Anyplace called The White Coffee Pot didn't stand a chance. The soda fountain intrigued, but the Italian Delight Restaurant, with its center seating below the mall floor was far too exotic, too worldly to pass up. While Tooey devoured a grilled cheese sandwich and French fries, his grandfather prattled on about how JFK attended the mall's opening ceremonies and so on and so on.

All Tooey knew was that his lunch was delicious, and that from their subfloor booth, if he timed things right, he could get a glimpse up the shorter skirts of the girls and women walking by.

He quit when his grandmother gave him that look.

Back then, Harundale Mall's holiday-mania comforted Tooey. Now the Bicentennial hoopla, the busy and crowded USA overload, plucked his nerves.

Tooey entered Read's Drugstore. The aisles were a gauntlet of customers stocking up on picnic and party paraphernalia along with their Gee Your Hair Smells Terrific shampoo and Ayds diet candy. A kindergartner wearing neither shoes, socks, nor a shirt lay on the floor, coloring.

Tooey put a toothbrush, an off-brand tube of toothpaste, and a can of spray deodorant in his basket. In the back, near the pharmacist's counter and a parking lot exit, was a magazine rack. Tooey picked up the most recent *National Lampoon* and a copy of *CREEM*.

A door marked 'Employees' opened. A girl came out. She walked by, smiling at Tooey like a delinquent. She smelled smoky, but not like cigarettes.

Two rowdy teenagers, maybe sixteen, along with a younger, chubbier rerun of the taller one, rounded the aisle. They were loud, jostling each other and roughhousing. The kid bumped a snooty-looking woman in an out-of-season hat. She complained and the three hellions snickered. They were hassling the pharmacy cashier to sell them a *Hustler* magazine, or at least a *Penthouse*, as Tooey walked away.

He got in line at the main checkout. The stoner bag-girl stood next to a fat cashier. They both wore smocks and nametags. The little old lady in front of Tooey smiled at him while they waited their turn to pay. She looked like she was a skinny friend of Andy Griffith's Aunt Bee, and he felt sorry for her having to shop here among the modern rabble. The three jerk kids got in line behind Tooey, each of them with several packages of Fourth of July sparklers.

Aunt Bee's pal stepped to the head of the line and the stoner gave Tooey her flirty smirk again. "Well, aren't you a fox," she said. "Find what you were looking for?"

"I, I… did. I did. Th-th-thank you."

The punks stopped dead and cocked their heads like someone blew a whistle only they and dogs could hear. Tooey felt his face go strawberry.

The girl took his basket and started unloading it on the counter. "Got yourself some reading material? I like *CREEM*. *Rolling Stone*, too, but this issue's got Paul Simon on the cover, and I'm not much on Paul Simon."

"Me... either."

You enlisting?"

"I... "

"Sometimes guys stop here on their way to the recruiting center."

"I... no, I'm not en-en... no." Out of his element, Tooey was already self-conscious about his backwater dialect and soft-spoken voice. His stutter tasted like iced embarrassment on a huge slice of humiliation cake.

The fat cashier told the old lady her total. As though it was a sluggish dawning surprise she might have to pay, the lady, with a palsy that worsened with each maneuver, opened her purse, her wallet, and her change pouch, and then started counting coins as if they might be coated with nitroglycerin. Maybe it was a con. Maybe old Miss Mayberry thought if she dawdled long enough, somebody would say don't worry, close enough. Either way, she took forever.

Tooey wanted Stoner Girl to say something to him. He prayed she wouldn't. He wanted to answer with a response that wouldn't make the situation more awkward. He knew that was impossible. His meager confidence slipped and fell out of the sky like D.B. Cooper without a parachute.

"Hey!" the fat cashier barked loud enough to startle Tooey and catch the attention of everybody within earshot. "You ready love-love-lover boy or did you want to stand there and stare at Grace Slick a few more minutes?"

The boys with the sparklers cracked up with foot-stomping, hand-clapping glee. Even Stoner Girl chortled. Fat Cashier took Tooey's money, and sent him packing with his purchases and a sincere regret he hadn't stayed his hick-ass home.

Tooey left the mall and drove north. He drove past cemeteries, car dealerships, and a drive-in theater. Highways and stoplights and traffic didn't come naturally to him. Tooey navigated water much better than asphalt.

He glanced at his mood ring, gray–black, whatever the hell that meant, and took a turn at the stoplight by mistake.

CHAPTER 9

Cherry Hill, one of Baltimore City's southernmost neighborhoods, was established for Negro veterans of World War II and Korea. Hemmed in by railroad tracks and the Patapsco River, by the middle of the 1970's its geographical isolation felt like a kill switch built into the community's short-lived promise. Cherry Hill was what frightened White people visualized when they talked about urban blight.

As Tooey rode in his wrong-turn redneck pickup, he got a sense the locals weren't used to seeing many people like him passing through. Men glared at him from rowhouse steps, and at the next light a group of kids on roller skates pointed him out to one another as they crossed the street in front of him. A dapper senior citizen on a bench outside a barbershop shook his head at Tooey.

Tooey wished he could tell them who he was and how he felt. For years during segregation, his maternal grandparents, now deceased, ran a pool hall for black men. The Kleggs were well respected for their business dealings. People of both races still often said that to Tooey. When she was a teenager, Tooey's grandmother once shoved a grown man out a second story window for what he called a black girlfriend of hers. Moviestar, who'd spent his life on the bay, knew men weren't separated by much out there. You either worked hard or you didn't. Nothing else.

Tooey was uncomfortable around the casual racism of many people he knew outside his family, but as he drove through Cherry Hill he couldn't shake the images that TV had imprinted on him during the Baltimore race riots of 1968. The people he'd seen on Channel 13 didn't seem like anyone he knew. They were the same on the outside, but there was something pushed to the brink in their eyes. He understood their anger. Martin Luther King had been murdered, they'd had enough. The explosion of rage made sense to Tooey even as a kid. Yet city Black people, if he were honest with himself, scared the piss out of him.

Approaching a park, he knew he was going to have to confront his fear. The unmistakable shaking of a front-end flat tire insisted.

Tooey got out and removed his jack and lug wrench from behind the truck's bench seat. His spare was underneath. He slid on his back and unscrewed the wing nut that held it to the truck's carriage. While on the ground, he scoped the park and saw that a group of men at maybe a hundred yards had stopped playing softball to watch him.

There was a cluster of brick row homes across the street with a lot of activity out front. Some kids were playing Mother, May I on the sidewalk and a group of ladies gathered around a table near the steps of the house at the end of the block.

As Tooey jacked the front of his truck he tried to stay aware of his surroundings. He couldn't help thinking how this would have never happened with his boat. Not the flat tire, of course, but a mechanical problem. Sure, he wasn't as diligent as his grandfather, Tooey didn't fix every issue as fast as or as skillfully as Moviestar would have, but he did keep the *Miss Ruth* in the vicinity of tip-top shape. He never broke down on the water. Was this proof he should stick with what he knew? When he got the tire fixed should he turn and head home? Cut his losses and spend his life on a workboat?

He wasn't sure what the answers were, but damned sure knew he wanted to get that tire changed double-time.

He saw three of the ballplayers, one with a bat, heading his way.

Two men, a few years older than Tooey, came out of the end-unit row house on the other side of the street. An elderly woman socializing out front called one of the men to her. She pointed to Tooey with her thumb. Those men walked toward him as well.

One of the ballplayers threw a rock. It pinged off the driver's side quarter panel with a metallic pop and a sharp ricochet. Tooey figured that if the rock were meant to hit him it would have.

The slighter of the two guys coming across the street, his walk reminded Tooey of James Coburn, yelled past the broken-down pickup and across the field. "No. Uh-uh!" he shouted. "Won't be none of that. Nothing here for you boys. You all stay over there and play your game." Tooey watched the trio turn and stroll back to the field.

"Need some help?" the big man, getting bigger, asked as they advanced. In his mind, Tooey named him Muscles.

"Uh... I, I think I got it, but thanks. Thanks."

Muscles bent down and picked up the four-ended spider wrench and stepped close while Tooey finished lifting the truck. The small dude lit a cigarette, leaned against a light pole, and said, "What the hell you doing down here? You lost?"

"Yeah, I, I guess. I was headed into the city."

Small dude laughed and said, "Well, you sure here now."

Tooey wasn't certain where to look, so he looked the man in the eye like he'd been taught. "I sure am," he said.

A little boy ran down the sidewalk to the man. The man grabbed the boy, tossed him in the air and caught him, the kid laughing all the time, the cig dangling out of the man's mouth.

"Whachoo doin', daddy?" the boy asked.

"We're giving this young man a hand, Troy."

"But *you* ain't doin' nothing," Troy said.

"Oh, I sure am, kid."

Muscles unscrewed the lug nuts and lifted the tire off the rim. Tooey put the spare on and his new friend began to hand-tighten the nuts back on. The man and his son watched the process.

Tooey stored his tools and shook both men's hands. "Thank you," he said. "I owe, owe you anything?"

"Not a problem," said Troy's father. "Now you want to turn around here and steer right back out to the highway. Where you from anyway?"

"Over on the Eastern Shore."

"You don't know nothing about 'round here then, do you?"

"I was just thinking the same thing myself."

"Might want to head on back where you come from."

"I was just thinking the same thing myself."

Instead of following the man's advice, once he drove away from Cherry Hill, Tooey turned north again, crossed the four-towered Hanover Street drawbridge, and drove into Baltimore.

Where he rode around lost for a good part of the next hour.

CHAPTER 10

Amy Ruari wanted to walk around the counter and kick him right where it hurts. Amy wasn't used to putting up with so many drunks. Her shift should have ended by now, but it was Friday, Fourth of July weekend, and Debbie, her relief, was running late again, probably loaded herself. Amy was working toward a tizzy trying to restock her station and wait on a line of customers all at the same time.

And there was this dork, kneading his chubby bulldog jowls and clogging the line in an attempt to change his order for the third time, but it was too late. Amy had his two large Polishes with all the colors wrapped and in the bag.

"That's two fifty," Amy said. "Come on, let's go. Next!"

The heavyset man in the wrinkled seersucker jacket knocked his soda over fumbling to pay, but he pulled it together and moved on so the next knucklehead could step up and annoy her.

"Big John with the works, a Polish with kraut, two fries, two Cokes."

"You got that, Keith?" Amy asked.

Keith was on the grill. Since graduation, Amy spent almost every day except Sundays with Keith. Keith never had much to say and that was fine with Amy.

Amy's father owned a diner a few neighborhoods away. She and her dad never spent more than ten minutes together without quarreling. He was a practical man, business-minded with no patience for anything he considered nonsense. Amy was an artist. Her father said that was code for hippie. She would call him Archie Bunker. He'd say Archie had it mostly right and as long as she was under his roof la la la. Amy would throw down her apron or the menus she was holding and storm out. And now she worked at the famous Polish Jack's on East Baltimore Street, on the one and only Block.

"Got it, Aim."

"Three twenty-five. Who's next? What can I get for you, sir?"

Amy disliked her job, but it got her out of the house, and she had performed well enough to have already gotten a raise. Tips were pretty good, too. She felt a connection to the neighborhood. Amy's favorite grandfather had been a vaudeville magician during The Block's golden age. She knew it was a far tawdrier place now, but Amy romanticized the early eras of Baltimore's notorious red light district. She'd drawn and painted scenes imagined from those days ever since she was a child.

The next customer teetered up and slurred, "What y' got?"

"Everything's there on the board," Amy said. "Want to step aside while you decide, sir, and I'll take care of the gentleman behind you."

"What's in your special sauce?" the slurrer wanted to know.

"It's a secret," Amy said. "Tomato, onion, and pepper."

"Hell of a secret. Your chili any good?"

"Sir." Amy's next breath came out in a poof. "I have no idea how you prefer your chili. I'm seventeen. I can't afford Art School. My father is never not pissed at me. It's July and it's humid as feet. I feel grodier every day. I'm not even sure I'm going to make it until the next shift comes in without vomiting. Now would you like to order or would you rather talk some more? Because there is more."

"Large Polish, fried onions and peppers."

"Next!"

A serious looking boy with chestnut blonde hair and an angled jaw-line stepped to the counter. He wore a three-toned brown short-sleeved pullover with a cream collar. His shoulders were wide, his chest thick. He stood straight.

"Are... are... you Amy?" he stammered. "I was told you, you could tell me where to find Dee Bradnox."

CHAPTER 11

Amy said, "You have to order. I can't stand here and talk to you."
Tooey couldn't take his eyes off Amy. Below all that Ann-Margret hair piled up and paper-hatted, complimented by a somehow charming sheen of perspiration on her brow and cheeks, were eyes the color of Tooey's favorite jeans. Her skin was light and freckled, her nose petite with a slight point toward the pearly gates.

Tooey stuttered. "I've never had a Pole, a Pole, a Polish sausage."

"Good for you," Amy said.

The trick was to try, but not too hard. Trying too hard risked disaster. "What's in the special sauce?" The question came out like Tooey hoped.

She rolled her eyes at him. "Soda? Fries?"

"Yes. Yes, please."

"Regular Polish, works. Got that Keith?"

"Got it, Aim."

"One fifty. Stand over there please until its ready." She looked past him. "Yes sir, can I help you?"

Self-conscious and befuddled, Tooey did what he was told. Amy handed him his order and said, "Go eat over there. My relief just came in."

⅄

Amy sat down next to Tooey at the end of the counter. She carried her purse and a fountain soda. "Hi," she said.

"Hi," Tooey said. He pointed at his meal. "Th-this is excellent."

"We sell a ton of them and you can only get them here." She sang, "Polish Jack that is my name, Polish Sausage that's my game."

"Well… good for you," Tooey couldn't help returning Amy's earlier zing.

Didn't faze her. She said, "You know. From the radio?"

He chewed and shook his head no.

"We have an annual sausage eating contest, too." Amy said. "We were in National Geographic last year."

"No kidding? Were, were you in the magazine?"

"No, but my drawings almost were." She pointed to the cartoon sandwiches and sides on the menu board.

"They're good." Tooey said, meaning it and relaxing. "Look, you got the little sears on the sausage and everything. Shows an eye for detail."

"Ah, you must be the acclaimed art critic…" It took a beat for Tooey to realize Amy was waiting for him to finish her sentence.

"T-Tooey Walter. Wesley. Wesley Walter, but everybody calls me Tooey."

She held out her hand and said, "Amy." He wiped his greasy mitt on his pants before shaking. "But you know that," she said.

"Hi, Amy."

"Heaven told me somebody might be coming to see her soon."

"Huh?"

"Oh, sorry," Amy said. "Heaven. That's Dee's stage name. Umm… where she works they use stage names."

"How y'all know each other?" Tooey almost couldn't imagine Amy in the same thought as Dee Bradnox.

"Dee's been coming in every few days as long as I've worked here. Always gets a Hot and Spicy and a Fresca. We talk, and out of nowhere one day, she tells me her real name. She's my age, right? A bit older, maybe. Not the youngest working The Block by far. It's gross, but they're kids sometimes, y'know?"

"How... how old are you?" Tooey asked.

"Just graduated high school. Catholic High Class of '76." She sipped her soda. "Now what, right? Ugh. I don't even want to think about it."

Amy had an accent unlike any Tooey knew existed. "Calf-lick?"

"You know, religious school. Nuns and stuff." Amy continued, "So Heaven—sorry again, Dee—stopped in the day before yesterday, or maybe the day before, and told me a friend might be coming to pick her up, and that he might come here to ask where to find her. She said that once she knew for certain when you'd be coming she'd let me know where to tell you she'd be."

"So... where is she?"

"That's the bad news I guess," Amy Ruari said, "I haven't seen her since."

Tooey offered Amy a ride, but she said she was fine. He tossed his trash in the wastebasket and was holding the door open for her. The cook behind the counter hollered, his hand cupped to his mouth, "Hey, Aim, can you come back here for a few more minutes? Debbie says she think she's going to be sick."

CHAPTER 12

Tooey's mood ring read grayish with yellow streaks. He had no idea what either color was supposed to say about his mood, but after meeting Amy he felt worlds better, so even though she wasn't much help, Tooey hit the bricks.

Amy wowed him for sure. Tooey thought she made the kind of impression that obligated a person to smile every time they remembered her. Yet, as he walked beyond The Block's fringes and in toward its heart, Tooey's instincts stopped him mid-stride, as if he were entering a predatory place like the marsh or woods. Places where it was important to know where he was stepping.

Everything eye-level glowed with an incandescent shimmer and pulsating neon hum, a multi-colored perpetual twilight that threw off Tooey's sense of time. He wondered when the moon and stars last managed to shine through down here.

Porno shops and strip joints dominated the landscape, with a few tattoo parlors and greasy spoons interspersed like contaminated islands in a flooded river of smut. Signs in storefront windows advertised everything from private movie booths to live XXX-rated peep shows to two-girl massage. Explicit promotional posters and girlie magazine covers displayed skin unfamiliar to Tooey's experience.

Groups of men, varying in age, numbers, and levels of drunken volume, crowded the pavement. Laughter and careening shenanigans surrounded Tooey, but the amusement felt aggressive, and the physical playfulness carried an unmistakable threat of hair-trigger violence. The air was thick with risk. Tooey smelled trouble and popcorn.

Doormen, hawkers, open-shirted guys with immense belt buckles and gold chains, stood in front of bars with names like Stage Door, Club Harem, and the Glass Slipper, pouncing on passers-by and shouting carnival barker style come-ons. "Don't miss the show, gentlemen! Right this way, right this way! Stripping like you like it: red hot, spicy, sizzling! Step right up – it's show time!"

Before gathering the nerve to enter, Tooey twice walked by the After Hours Club, the queen of The Block's one time glamorous reputation. There was no doorman on duty.

Tooey descended a flight of steps to an alcove where the Orioles were playing on the TV behind a small bar. An old man sat alone and watched the game, smoking and drinking a beer, and not bothering to return Tooey's greeting. Tooey walked down a second set of stairs that, even though he was Methodist, reminded him of the circles of hell.

A horseshoe bar and a propeller-shaped stage dominated the center of the darkened lower level room. A rugged stripper wearing caked-on makeup and gold panties twirled in a bored do-se-do for the handful of men who sat staring into her crotch.

This was it? Where was Starr Flame, the woman Tooey read of in flea market magazines, "the siren farm girl with the curves galore and bouffant hair-do who delights audiences"? Was there any way possible this hole in the wall could be where "The Hottest Flame in Burlesque" performed her famous routines?

Instead of the glitz he expected, Tooey got treated to the unenthusiastic, intoxicated twirlings of a middle-aged woman who might have resembled Cher if he were to squint and bang himself on the head with an oar a few times. With no sign of Dee Bradnox, or anything else he wanted to see, Tooey headed out. As he passed, the white haired fellow watching the game said, "You looking for something?"

"Sir?"

"You look like somebody looking for something different than most."

"A friend," Tooey said. "I'm... I'm looking for a friend."

Sol introduced himself. A waitress came by, and with a, "Hey, Katie, get me a couple," Sol ordered two National Bohemians. The beer was ice cold.

"Can you believe these shitting-ass Birds?" Sol asked. "Lost four in a row to Boston, then last night to the Tigers. They do it again tonight, they go on the road looking like dummies."

Tooey eased onto his barstool, "After they got over that losing streak, I thought they were going to be all right." Moviestar enjoyed talking baseball, so Tooey did too.

Sol looked at Tooey and nodded agreement. They watched the game in silence and drank beer.

"You wor-work here?" asked Tooey.

"Used to once," Sol said.

"Did you know Starr Flame?"

"Still do. She bought this joint. Comes in sometimes. Still can't get enough attention. Still doing her thing, as they say. Course, fewer and fewer of anybody cares what her thing's doing."

"What was she like back when...when people did care?" Tooey asked.

"Man," Sol said, "Starr used to come from behind the curtain in a gown and leopard skin cape with its paws wrapped around her. She'd strut up and down that runway lighting candles, carrying a single rose she put in her mouth while she peeled. She'd throw that rose, a treasure to somebody in the audience. Some other guy would get to powder her ass and that was even better.

"Laying back on her long scarlet couch, she'd push a button and smoke would rise between her legs. Lengths of silk and lace waved like fire." Sol smiled and shook his head. "She'd heat 'em up alright," he said. "Leave the stage to cheers. And like a real showbiz pro, a lady, she would get dressed in her fancy gowns, and come out and work the room. You know, circulate; talk to the public. That's why she was a star, Bawlmer's mascot. None of this take your titties out, shake your hooch in somebody's face, and hustle drinks. In my day, there'd be none of that." Sol wet his whistle.

"She had a presence, boy-o, flair. Weren't none ever better, no sir."

The O's scored a run at the bottom of the third off an Al Bumbry single, but it should have gotten them two. Brooks was tagged out at home and Sol slapped the bar for it.

Tooey asked, "You...you been around here a while, huh?"

"The After Hours Club was Bawlmer's Ritz, man. Politicians, athletes, movie stars, all of them came through here. Some of the most gorgeous women in the world took their clothes off on that stage down there. There'd be musicians playing behind the curtain, and the girls would come out and put on their shows. It was first-class."

"How long you been on The Block?"

"When I was a boy," said Sol, "Prohibition wasn't nothing. The Block ran wide open. Vaudeville, dancing girls, scratch houses. I used to sell roasted peanuts with my father from a cart. There were performers up and down the street. Michelangelo was an organ grinder with a monkey, and his monkey, Pierre, was a pickpocket."

"No kidding? A pickpocket?"

"They used it in their act, you know, but every once in while some rube's wallet would come up missing and everybody'd figger Pierre got him." Sol laughed. "Saturday nights were something right through the thirties. People would come out, dressed to the nines even in tough times. We had all the finest restaurants down here. Top acts headlined these places—Abbott and Costello, Jackie Gleason, Gypsy Rose Lee. The Gayety was top of the line, one of the ace theaters in the country. Old Hon Nickles used to own it. Place is a dump now."

"Is…there anything around here that isn't?"

"Nah, guess not," Sol conceded, staring at his bottle of beer.

"Bad news right? Drugs, p-p-prostitution, muggings. All that?"

Sol pondered the question. "Old man Cohan ran things for a long time. After the war, The Block went all the way to Charles Street and the Boss kept a lid on things. He met in the back room once a month with the chief of police, a rep from the DA's office, the city councilmen. Everybody kept mutual respect.

"Then the Lord Cornwall came into the picture," Sol said. "Led everybody his way for a few years. Things started getting more lowdown. I wouldn't go so far to say The Block was still classy, but it wasn't a craphole yet either."

"What happened?" Tooey asked as Detroit tied it up in the top of the fifth.

"People got worse, I guess. The Lord got hisself got, busted, and then got hisself disappeared. Cocaine cowboys rolled in, started doing business different. Selling drugs right over the bar. Twelve year old runaways from the county soliciting undercover johns in the peeps."

"So the cops…?"

"Police station right down the street." Sol pointed with his beer. "Half of them part of any problem. Corrupt as politicians. You know the mayor's office overlooks this street? Bawlmer boys stick together. The Feds, though? Feds are a whole different story.

"The Feds busted the Lord Cornwall and everything the bosses kept under control spilled out like an avalanche. Chaos. All that dope.

And porno. Porno was the final nail in the coffin of the old ways. Like the movies killed vaudeville, porno killed The Block."

"Looks like The Block's doing all right." Tooey said. "Lot of money out there."

"That porno is cancer, buddy, an aggressive, billion dollar a year cancer."

A tall man with a funeral parlor complexion and long hair tied in a ponytail entered the alcove from a back hallway. He stepped to Sol with a tumbler of brown liquor in one shaking hand and a cigarette in the other.

"Bouncer got in an altercation earlier," Sol said. "Cleared the place out. This is Dr. Henry Merriman." Sol turned on his barstool. "Bronco going to be okay, doc?"

"Eight stitches." The doctor looked like he could use a doctor.

"This young man," Sol told Dr. Henry Merriman, "this one's a friendly fellow. Not from here." Sol pulled a wad of cash from his hip pocket and thumbed loose a few bills. The doctor took them, finished his drink, stubbed out his smoke, and gave Tooey an apathetic nod on his way out.

"Eh," Sol shrugged, "enough of all this geezer rigmarole. Tonight, you should be out there making some history of your own."

"What's the best way to find somebody? A particular dancer?"

"Ask around. Most of these peelers take shifts in two or three places a night if they can get away with it. Owners and managers used to give a damn who they hired. Now, long as they got some beaver on stage, what do they care if it just wobbled over from the joint next door?"

"Know a girl named Heaven?"

Sol chuckled. "I've known many a girl I thought was Heaven, but nobody goes by that name works here. Here's a tip. Befriend the bartenders, not some sad old ghost sitting alone watching a baseball game he could go to if he really gave a damn. Bartenders, man. Bartenders hold the keys to the world."

Rising to leave, Sol said, "You know, though, I think about how things really were, those old times weren't all that different than now. This whole part of town's never been nothing but tits, jazz, and wrong-doing. Illegal card games and backroom blowjobs. You had the moola you always could buy any high you wanted. The recipe for The Block is two parts booze to one part pussy with a splash of menace and a twist of despair." He placed a ten spot on the bar. "I guess no matter how much us fogeys might want to sentimentalize, The Block has always been a pit of vile quicksand preying on the weakness of men for a lousy goddamn dollar." Sol raised his beer bottle.

"Thank you, lord, amen," he said before finishing off what was left.

Chapter 13

Tooey checked half a dozen bars in a row, talked to a bartender in each club, and drank some of six beers. The sausage sandwich settled in his stomach like a shipwreck. Not a single bartender knew Heaven or recognized the girl in the Polaroid, even after Tooey caught on to the art of better tipping.

Discouraged, Tooey took a detour into a massive circus-themed porn shop. The glassed-in cashier's stall was helmed by a man with a boil on the side of his head the size of a toddler's fist. A steady line of customers exchanged bills for coins and tokens.

Following signs promising live action upstairs, Tooey navigated through the herd to a circle of doors. Each door provided privacy to a snug closet with a seat and phone, a small light, and a full-length window with a purple curtain on the other side of the glass.

Tooey dropped six tokens into a metal box on the wall and the draperies rose on a slinky blonde, as attractive as the best looking stripper he'd seen that night. Surrounding her was a collection of one-way mirrors in the round. As soon as any curtain fell it rose again. The girl's bed rotated and she was talking on the phone, maybe to somebody on the other side of one of those other mirrored windows, but as far as

Tooey knew she could be conversing with anybody from her folks to Phyllis Diller.

Tooey liked watching the girl touch herself. When time was up and his curtain came down, he forced himself to leave. He went back outside, crossed at the corner, and made a U-turn back into the sea of debauchery that flowed along The Block's sidewalks.

The street barkers all looked dressed from the same wardrobe. They were jewelry-laden, decked out in polyester shirts with mammoth collars and leisure suits of colors otherwise found only in animated movies. Many wore mirrored aviator sunglasses. At night. Quite a few possessed that special something. There was Cross-eyes, Wolfman, and Billy Jack Hat. There was the dude with one arm, the dude with the lisp, then the dude named Levi who referred to himself in the third person.

Levi happened to catch Tooey's eye. "Hey, hermano, why don't you walk in take a look, see somethin' good?" He clicked his tongue and winked. "Beautifulest ladies right inside. Levi never steer you wrong. Step this way, ge'men, show's always just startin'."

The girls were prettier down here, the clientele younger. Three strippers in various stages of undress were working the stage behind the bar. As Tooey approached, a man careened away from his barstool. The bartender was right there, picking up her tip money and wiping the bar with a towel.

Long straight black hair with an Indian princess complexion, slim but curvy, the bartender wore second-skin jeans and a sleeveless leather vest.

Tooey ordered a longneck. A bargirl in a glittery halter-top that accentuated every swing of her unrestrained jugs came fishing, asking Tooey to buy her a drink. He declined, she asked for a dollar for the jukebox. Tooey gave it to her and she went away.

The bartender came back. Tooey waved her over. "Uh, hi," he said. "I'm luh-looking… for a friend of mine and I was wondering if you might, might... know her." He slid a ten dollar bill toward the bartender and she took it.

"What's her name?" the bartender leaned across the bar to be heard over the disco booming over the sound system.

"It's Dee, but I guess they call her Heaven. I've got a p-picture," he said.

"Let me see."

"Any help?"

"I know her," the bartender said. "Used to dance here but her boy-friend tried to get more money out of us. Owner told them both to hit the road."

"A-any idea where I can find her?"

"Why?"

"Her... her daddy died." Tooey put out another ten.

The bartender's sympathetic response to Tooey's lie intensified her beauty. It didn't keep her from taking his money. Tooey sipped his beer.

"This time of night on a Friday, try Nick's Mousetrap," said the bartender.

An older woman, dressed for business, walked behind the bar and spoke to the bartender. Tooey heard the woman say somebody had to leave. The bartender asked if he needed anything else right now because, "I'm going to go ahead and dance a set."

Tooey shook his head. The naked girl on stage gathered the clothing she'd shed and the dollar bills she'd earned for doing so, and stepped down from the runway. Tooey's bartender stepped up. Those funky first guitar notes of "Tell Me Something Good" started playing. Chaka Kahn started singing. The bartender started dancing.

The bartender shut her eyes and swayed her shoulders. She bent at the waist and put her hands on her knees. Her lower half started moving. She opened her eyes. A light switch had flipped on behind them. Tooey noticed goose bumps on her arms.

The bartender snapped open the top of her vest and smiled at her enraptured audience. She could have asked each of them for a hundred dollars per button, and they'd have come up with the money somehow. The tip of her tongue poked out. She bit her bottom lip. She lowered her eyes and unfastened her jeans.

When the song ended the bartender wore pink ankle socks, black lace panties, and her unbuttoned vest. "Fire" by the Ohio Players came on and her energy obliged the other two dancers to raise their game. The bartender danced with such natural joy, for a few moments it all seemed like good clean fun. There were yells of "God Bless America" mixed in with all the "take it off" shouts.

The singer told the bartender to shake what you got and she did. She caressed her breasts under her vest, and by the end of the verse she was slipping her leather aside. Her knuckles alone covered her nipples. When she took the vest all the way off, like shedding a layer of flesh, she turned and smiled at Tooey.

Tooey shivered, and shot off in his corduroys.

⋏

Tooey finished his beer in shock and indignity. On his way out of the bar, the bartender stopped pulling her panties down long enough to wave and mouth the words, "good luck." Donna Summer moaned all over the sound system.

Outside, Levi said, "Where you goin', m'man? Levi not tell you right? Come on now, don't let dem Hushpuppies a yours walk you into makin' a mistake, my brother."

CHAPTER 14

Tooey shuffled away in self-disgust. To clean his mess, he ducked into a filthy bathroom at a place that sold sliders by the bag.

Afterwards, he walked next door to Nick's Mousetrap. He was inside and sitting down at an empty high top table before the doorman could even open his mouth. A pretty waitress with a vast Day-Glo Afro took Tooey's order for a beer he had no intention of drinking.

Tooey's front corner perch was as secluded as any seat in a titty bar could be. The bargirls were working the room. They'd swarmed every joint he'd been in. A few were dancers too, but not all. In skimpy lingerie and easily pulled aside bikinis, they were always next to naked. Their job was to coax customers into spending every nickel.

Buying one of the bargirls a watered-down Champale cost twenty dollars. After a round of crotch-grabbing, the girl would try to get the customer to buy her friend a drink, too. Maybe a trip to an upstairs room. Tooey had seen it throughout the evening. A skinny blonde in unbuttoned and unzipped cutoffs approached. Tooey gave her nothing except an understated shake of the head. She sneered at him before turning to a group of foreign sailors at a nearby table.

The woman on stage stood under a disco ball with her back to the audience. She wore a kimono over panties over curvy hips and grasped the brass pole with one hand. She made dreamy but dull eye contact with her audience in the wall-sized mirror she gazed into. She peeled the kimono back, looked over her bare shoulder with much-practiced seduction. She turned back to the mirror and the garment fell to the runway. With something close to grace, she reached behind and unclasped her bra. Her breasts were what Tooey imagined a first girlfriend's might look like.

Tooey could feel himself growing erect again.

That was it, he'd had enough. He was tired, half drunk, and had blown a load in his pants once already. He wasn't going to find Dee Bradnox tonight. Maybe he'd come back tomorrow. Maybe he wouldn't. Tooey stood to leave.

And that was when the emcee announced, "Gentlemen, while the tantalizing Tina gets ready for her third dance, give a round of applause for Goldie leaving the rear stage, and put your hands together for your favorite, our own little piece of heaven, Heaven!"

Chapter 15

Earlier that evening, getting ready for work in her boxy studio apartment, Dee had laid her clothes out across her metal-framed cot.

Tonight, Heaven, a name Salt had christened her with, would wear candy apple green pleather boots, a canary Lycra top, and hot pants with a G-string underneath. The nails on her fingers and toes were painted aquamarine. She wasn't yet sure which of her various styled and colored wigs she would choose.

Dee resembled her mother with long sandy hair and longer legs tanned brown. She wasn't bonkers for the gap between her front teeth or the way her ears stuck out, but she knew how to work what she'd been blessed with.

What had stopped working a while back was her stint as a groupie.

Dee had called her father from the Baltimore bus station. He said, "I told you you're never welcome back here, Delores. That has not changed." He hung up on her, and she made a beeline to The Block. It wasn't Dee's first time taking off her clothes in front of a crowd. At least now, she was making money at it.

She couldn't pinpoint meeting Salt Wade; he was just one of those guys who was always hanging around the clubs. She started fucking him for coke. As soon as he became her "manager" he started trying to pimp her. The pressure was mounting; he'd become far less nice than he used to be, and he was never that nice to start with.

"What do you see in that guy, anyway?" her co-worker Orchid asked.

"Great drugs, lots of money, and a huge dick."

"Ah, the three prerequisites." They both laughed.

Dee liked the way Salt looked. He was stocky, country boy strong. After all the musicians she'd screwed, it was nice being with a man who didn't feel so fragile. She found Salt's baby-alligator smile fascinating.

His voice was deep, with that southern rhythmic charm.

Okay, so the hair was bad. He wore a helmet of reddish brown hay, cowboy boot-themed sideburns, and a Joe Namath moustache. Salt thought he looked like the porn star that looked like Burt Reynolds.

He stared at people like a creepy owl.

One night, Dee talked Salt into having dinner in Little Italy. Dee had crammed down enough home-style fried fish, fried chicken, turnip greens, and biscuits in recent weeks to satisfy a lifetime. She needed a meal in a real restaurant, but Salt was amped all night, kept disappearing into the bathroom, drank lots of wine, and ate almost nothing.

He was rattling on about some fossilized Blues singer he saw once in a Memphis hotel when he caught a smile passed between Dee and their waiter.

"It's rude not to look at a person when they're talking," Salt said.

"Sorry," Dee said. "I'm listening,"

"Oh, no," Salt protested. "Something more interesting over there, go for it."

"What are you talking about, Salt? I'm paying attention. I don't have to laser beam you with my eyes to hear you."

"So you gonna listen to me but rubberneck Frankie Avalon over there all night?" Salt's ruddy complexion bloomed burgundy. When he got a head of steam going, his skin splotched and he sweated musk cologne.

"Are you kidding me?' she asked. "You're trying to persuade me to sell my ass, but you're upset I glanced at a waiter? Are you out of your mind?"

"Didn't look so glancing." Salt's pout carried threat.

"If anything, I was commiserating with him," she said.

"What the hell's that supposed to mean? Commiserating?"

"He's brought you great food all night and you've pooh-poohed it like it came out of a can. You've got two different meals sitting there in front of you, neither of them touched."

"I didn't know if I'd like the veal or the chicken and you know what? I don't like either fucking one of 'em." His volume and tone alone earned the hushed attention of the other diners.

"You want me to eat? That the problem?" Salt stuffed a garlic roll into his mouth. "And don't commiserate with nobody over me," he said. "You don't like something, go back wherever you come from, to that daddy who don't want you."

That's what she got for sharing her feelings one time. One damned time.

"Look me in the eye," Salt demanded.

"Fuck you, you moonshine drinking goat-fucker."

Salt wasn't usually as thin-skinned as he turned out to be that night.

Back at his place, Salt choked Dee until she blacked out. She stayed with Orchid a few days after that, afraid to go back to her own dump apartment. No one else knew where Orchid lived, and if they did, even Salt would think twice before raising ruckus in her neighborhood.

A week or so later, with a new shipment of good coke in hand, Salt visited Dee at work, and she went back home with him.

Then the cigar box came into Salt's possession.

The case wasn't an actual cigar box. It resembled one in design but was larger, made of metal, and not without weight. There was a handle like a workman's lunch box and a gold plated lock. A raised logo design showed two dogs barking at the moon, one sporting a barbed tail and holding a devil's trident. There was a recurring rattlesnake motif.

Salt could not shut up about his new case even though he was scared to death someone would steal it. Kept telling everybody the case was filled with the most valuable things in the world. Dee was thinking diamonds. Salt's paranoia had gotten so intense, in the last week he'd taken to sometimes chaining the case to his wrist. Salt told her the contents of his case were "worth more than anything you'll ever own in your life." Salt didn't know Dee's privileged background. Her parents spent more on nothing than most people did on everything.

Dee called her father once she'd made up her mind to steal Salt's treasure. Her father was far more receptive to her potential return than she'd anticipated.

Short of murder, Dee Bradnox tried every tactic she could think of to separate Salt Wade from his precious case.

One night Dee got Salt plastered on rye whiskey and crushed benzos she got from the doctor, but when they kicked in and he landed face first on the floor, she found that in his last conscious minutes he'd hidden the case. She tore his apartment apart looking for it, and had to put everything back the best she could before he awoke.

She talked that dirt-bag doorman Levi into mugging Salt, but he backed out once he realized who she was talking about robbing.

She put eye drops in Salt's barbecue and slaw. He spent the night in the bathroom. The case stayed with him.

She got Salt coked up and tried to screw him stupid enough to share whatever was in the case with her. It didn't work. Salt might've been a deranged hillbilly, but he was not stupid.

Now here it was Friday and time was running out.

Her father had said "by Monday".

She dry-swallowed a Quaalude.

When Dee Bradnox was fourteen, she lost her virginity to a much older boy. She got pregnant. Her father arranged an abortion. Dee might have looked like her mother, but until that spring she'd always been daddy's girl.

She needed to find a way to be that again.

Dee knew she was impulsive. She could be stubborn beyond reason. But she was smart, and strong, and she knew how to take a punch.

She told herself that she was sweet to the aged and to lost dogs, and though she was capable of saying the meanest things in the heat of a moment, she would not tolerate cruelty in others. She believed she possessed good traits, things she might pass on to a child someday, given another chance.

Chapter 16

The Orioles won and Nick's Mousetrap was packed. Dee was at the back of the room, where the dancers congregated between sets. She was surprised to see Tooey come in and take a seat upfront. Orchid brought him a beer. What was he doing here already?

Dee was working a group of rowdies; a couple of the group she knew to be undercover narcs. The one standing by the bar, the drunken loud-mouthed one with the preposterous perm and the Hawaiian disco shirt, had been particularly aggressive. He kept trying to force his hand into her short shorts.

"C'mon, baby, why don't you and me find a nice place to go be together?" His breath was hot and his words were garbled. "Just us," he said as he grazed her leg again.

"First there's not a nice place within five blocks of here, and second you know we can't do that. That's illegal."

"It's only illegal," the plainclothes inebriate said, "when we get caught."

"Buy me a drink?" Dee went back to the script.

"Sure, where's the waitress?"

"I go on soon. Maybe you get me a drink after. We'll spend some time."

"You got it," he said. He swayed over to where his friends held court.

Salt walked in holding the case. It was not chained to his wrist.

Salt spotted her across the crowded room. She stepped to the tanked plainclothes narc just as the emcee called her name and invited everybody to give her a round of applause.

Dee stood close. The narc had a drink in each hand. She tippy-toed to whisper to him and their bodies compressed into one. She kissed his ear, and said, "Keep your hands off me, wormhole." Then she pinched the tip of his cock as hard as she could and twisted.

The narc yelled, dropped his drinks, and tried to back away, but the only way that was happening was if he didn't want to take his entire penis with him. He reared his arm back, and whacked Dee with his open hand. He almost floored her. Salt leapt through the air, landing on the narc like a hayseed jungle cat. The case was still in Salt's grasp when he and the narc hit the deck.

The impact knocked the air out of both men. Satellite fights broke out. Within seconds Nick's Mousetrap was in pandemonium, and right in the middle of it all, Dee knelt, reached through the crowd of bodies tangled on the floor, and pried back every finger on Salt's left hand.

CHAPTER 17

It was Dee Bradnox. Tooey was sure. There she was, right where the too-beautiful stripping bartender told Tooey she'd be. Tooey had difficulty believing his own eyes. Until that point his search for Dee had seemed more like a wild goose chase than something that might actually get accomplished.

Tooey left his beer at the table. Even from this distance in a cramped bar, even in her laughable getup, he could see how pretty Dee still was. She was talking to some curly haired, Sonny Corleone-looking guy. Tooey had forgotten Dee's expressive, always-on-the-move eyebrows. Those eyebrows were clocking overtime now. Did she just look at him and smile? Tooey thought so.

A man in a hurry, carrying an etched metal case, bumped past Tooey. The man turned sideways to get through the throng. He reminded Tooey of a blue crab.

Tooey saw Dee press into Sonny Corleone. Sonny's eyes popped. Drinks flew, Sonny slapped Dee. Tooey started shoving people aside to come to Dee's rescue, but the man with the case broke through first. The man jumped Sonny Corleone and they both went crashing down.

Fights broke out all around. Bystanders at the center of the fray, friends of the Corleone family it appeared, pulled at the man with the case, while others concentrated on punching and kicking him. They were ganging up on the man for defending Dee. Tooey wanted to help. He grabbed and spun the first assailant he reached, a bald-headed man in a sport coat, and aiming for the nose, Tooey threw the first real swing of his adult life. The bald man's blood spurted and he tottered backwards, his arms flailing.

On the far side of the barroom, Tooey saw Dee break for a side door. She was carrying the crab-man's case. Tooey started to follow, but one of Sonny Corleone's cronies tried to latch on to him. That attacker missed, but somebody else's gut-punch landed like a cannonball. Tooey's air and balance left him in an instantaneous huff.

He buckled but did not fall. The baldie in the blazer rose to his knees, and reached for Tooey's arm from the edge of the brawling heap. Tooey noticed a thick leather lanyard around the man's neck. There was a badge attached. Shaking the baldheaded undercover cop loose, Tooey scanned the melee around him for his most promising escape route.

He wanted to pursue Dee, but trying to get to the side door was rife with opportunities to wind up cornered. Tooey scrambled for the teeming front exit.

There was a shout, "Police! Police! Nobody move a goddamned muscle!" and a stampede of men bolted toward the doors.

As Tooey attempted to join the charge, the bald cop he'd been fighting again reached out, and this time snagged Tooey's pants leg. Tooey fell, rolled, flipped onto his back – and kicked The Block's version of Kojak right in the face.

CHAPTER 18

Tooey flushed out into the street with everybody else. He was the one stumbling east, spewing Polish sausage and what felt like a quarter keg of beer.

Tooey drove until he saw a vacancy sign.

"One night?" The desk manager of the Mohawk Motor Inn asked. "If you want more you better pay now. We'll be full-up tomorrow."

"Make it two then." Tooey wasn't optimistic.

With a disinterest so passive it bordered on aggressive, the manager took a fifty and handed Tooey a key. The room was on the second of two courtyard floors. An almost full parking lot buffered the motel from the busy city causeway.

Sitting in a folding aluminum chair on the walkway balcony next to Tooey's room was a young guy with a six-pack of Schlitz, a smoke in his mouth, and a guitar on his lap. He had on blue jeans, but was barefoot and shirtless. His hair was black as raven feathers.

"Hey, man," the guy said, "how's it going? Wanna drink a beer with me?"

Tooey struggled with his door key. "No, no thanks."

"Your loss, chief."

Tooey took a long shower. He washed some parts three, four times. He brushed his teeth and sat on the bed in his underwear, his heart still pounding. He cranked open the humid room's one window. He counted his money. He walked over, popped the television on, went and sat back down. Tooey looked at his mood ring. Red and pink.

The television was too loud and lacked much to offer. The local news guy prattled on about upcoming Bicentennial Fourth of July ceremonies and celebrations. Tooey thought the broadcaster acted far more excited than what the times called for.

Part of the report was about Johnny Carson's sidekick, Ed McMahon, unveiling a giant national birthday cake at Fort McHenry Saturday night. The cake was shaped like America and weighed thirty tons, the biggest in the world, the reporter said. A barge would bring the cake up the Patapsco River to where Francis Scott Key wrote the Star Spangled Banner. A fireworks reenactment of the historic garrison's 1812 bombing was scheduled for midnight. Tooey guessed a pigpen dessert and a talk show ass-kisser were better than the thousands of rampaging British troops who were in town the last time the fort made news.

Tooey stood to change channels and turn down the volume. Channel 2 was playing *Fail Safe*, a thriller portraying accidental nuclear war. Eleven showed *Anna and the King of Siam*. Twenty had on a horror flick, 45 a John Ford western. Tooey turned the TV off, put on clean Lees and his Cheap Trick T-shirt, and went out on the balcony.

Not knowing what else to say, Tooey said, "Still offering one of those beers?" ·

"Sure, partner." The kid seemed glad to see Tooey return. "Pull that other chair out here. Sit down and have a brew. Good deal."

Once Tooey got seated, the kid held out his hand and said, "Willy Nelson."

"What?"

"Not that one, but I do come from Texas, too."

"T-Tooey Walter."

"Nice meeting you, Walter." Willy Nelson handed Tooey a beer. "What you been up to this fine summer evening?"

Tooey couldn't help but chuckle. "Man, you don't, you don't want to know."

"I'm a good listener."

"N-not... much of a talker."

"I hear ya, brother."

Willy Nelson drank his beer. Tooey held his and watched the busy street activity from the balcony's vantage point. Back home, Tooey would have been asleep for hours by now. Hard to believe it was past twelve and that many people were still out and about. In a breath, Tooey realized how exhausted he was.

Willy Nelson said, "Tasty, huh?"

"Huh? Oh, yeah, sorry. Somewhere else, head's not on straight."

"Wish mine wasn't. You got any speed? That's my favorite. You?"

"Me what?"

"You like speed?"

"Don't know. Nev-never tried it."

Willy Nelson's eyes widened. "What? Never? Aw, man, that's wacko."

"Yeah, I guess. You want money on the beer?"

"Nah, I'll getcha later."

"What, what about you?" Tooey asked. "What've you been doing tonight?"

"Just sitting here. Been stuck a few days. My old lady stranded me. Been thinking I might steal a car and get the hell out of Ball-tee-more, Walter."

"Don't steal mine."

"Which one's yours?"

"The pickup."

"Ha! Shoulda' guessed. Ahh, don't get uptight about it. I ain't ready to fly quite yet. Where'd you get that accent?"

"My granddad. Why you sticking around?"

"Hoping I might see the fireworks from here tomorrow night." Willy Nelson lit a cigarette, offered Tooey the pack while saying, "Like to get me a piece of that big ol' cake I been hearing about, too. I don't think I'm gonna get much else of what anybody ever promised, I damn sure would dig a chunk of birthday cake."

"They're not giving it away. They're selling it by the slice."

"So there you go."

They sat quiet. Willy Nelson never touched one guitar string.

"You look worried, Walter."

"I was. Now I-I'm just pissed. Well, pissed and a little sick to my stomach."

"And a little bit scared, maybe. You look a little scared."

"Yeah. Yeah, maybe."

"Well, sometimes being scared's what makes sense. If everything's handcarting it to hell, only a moron wouldn't get scared."

"What about, about you, Willy Nelson? What are you scared of?"

"Nothing," Willy Nelson laughed. "But I'm a big moron. Hey, man, why you think they got a motor court in the middle of Ball-tee-more called the Mohawk?"

Back in his room, television was still a dud. A commercial came on for Mr. Ray's Hairweave, followed by a karate school ad where an adorable Korean kid said, "Nobody bodders me," and another one said, "Nobody bodders me eeder," and winked. Tooey turned the black and white set off and lay down. The bed was lumpy as a gravel pit.

Tooey looked through his magazines. *Lampoon* had Fat Elvis on the cover. Tooey didn't find much inside to laugh at. He turned off the light and lay awake. He was determined now to see this thing with the Bradnoxes through. Maybe it was the fight and his narrow getaway. Maybe it was seeing Dee run off. Whatever the reason, Tooey Walter collapsed into sleep that night as resolute as he had ever been of anything.

CHAPTER 19

L ate Saturday morning, Tooey parked a few streets away and walked to The Block. He ate a diner breakfast, and passed a park where adults relaxed and kids scurried around like pint-sized crazy people. A group of codgers played cards. Nobody was drinking, or stripping, or as far as Tooey could tell, making a mess in their pants. If he was going to find Dee, he had to go back to a world where those things happened, but at that moment it was nice to see a pleasurable side of the city, a side that felt like real life.

Tooey, concerned over being identified for his part in last night's fracas, bought an Orioles baseball cap. He strolled past, then turned back, and entered a discount store offering jewelry, cameras, and luggage.

Clientele milled about and the lone cashier on duty was occupied with a sale. Tooey's turn came. He stepped up and said, "I want to buy a watch."

"Cool," the cashier said. "What kind?"

"Wrist."

The cashier was a bantam white boy with a Michael Jackson head of hair. He showed Tooey several options in the twenty-dollar range. Tooey picked out one on a brown leather band. Before the cashier rang up Tooey's purchase, Tooey noticed a stack of mood ring charts beside the register and asked, pointing, "Can, can I have one of those?"

"One of what?"

"A chart. I bought this ring, but don't know what the c-colors mean."

"I can only give you one of those if you buy a mood ring."

"But... like I said, I have a mood ring. I just don't have a chart."

"You didn't buy that ring here."

"But I'm getting ready to buy that watch from you."

"But it's not a mood watch."

"You got mood watches?"

Tooey registered red on his mood ring. His new mood wristwatch was yellow with streaks of charcoal. His handy new chart said neither was all that good.

⋏

Tooey stopped at a corner telephone booth.

"Hey, Pops!"

"Hey, sonny boy." Tooey could tell Moviestar was happy to hear his grandson's voice. "Whachoo doin'?"

"Up here trying to catch Dee Bradnox."

"She don't want to get caught, huh?"

"Yeah, I'm not sure what's going on, but I'm going to do what I came to do."

"There you go." A pause. "Everything okay?"

"Yes sir, everything's fine. Slept in a nice hotel and ate good. I think it's just a matter of miscommunication I haven't got with Dee yet. I'm hoping on doing that soon. I'd love to think I'd be home this afternoon or evening, tonight at the latest. What're you doing?"

"Not much. Might take the boat out for a spin. I wasn't for it this morning."

"Don't mess with that motor. She's running fine. You take her out today, and I'll fix what needs fixing Monday afternoon."

"Aye, aye, cap'n," Moviestar teased.

"You're too much, old man. What about Ma?"

"Your grandmother, she laid down, taking a nap."

Tooey's antennae went up. "That's rare. She feelin' alright?"

"Oh yes, just tired and got nothing on her schedule."

"Good for her. She's the hardest worker in the house."

"You got that right. Well, listen, I'm going to get ready and ride on down the shore. Be careful up there now. "

"Under control, Pops," Tooey lied.

"Alright then. Love you boy."

"Love you too, Pops. See you soon."

Even in broad daylight The Block was covered in sleaze. Tooey kept one thought moored, "If nobody knows you, you can be anybody." The idea had been delivered overnight by steamboat in a Mohawk Motor Court, burned-out dream.

⅄

Amy said, "I'm not even supposed to be here today."

"I'm glad you are though. Has, has Dee been in?"

"I was supposed to have the day off." Amy talked faster than anybody. "I've got to go to this street party thing we're having in our neighborhood this evening. And my mother wants me to make cupcakes and take my sister shopping for a dress – all this before five and they call me in this morning to open because Keith got drunk at the Rhapsody disco last night and fell down a flight of stairs and…"

Tooey walked Amy to her car. Her hair was down and loose, as natural and flowing as the tide, fiery as Old Bay seasoning. He could see the shyest of freckles on her oyster shell shoulders. Amy's eyes fascinated him. Her lips were as smooth as yacht club linen, moving non-stop, her voice soothing despite her thick Baltimore accent wound tight.

"…I'm getting tired of being the responsible one here," Amy was saying. "I'm seventeen. I told my boss this morning. I'm not getting anything extra for covering everybody else's rear ends all the time. What are they going to do in the fall if, when, I go to school? Who's going to be around to get called in on their day off and actually come in? What's your name again?"

"Tooey."

"Are you going to do it, Tooey? Are you going to come down here and open up on your day off?"

"Pruh-probably not."

"That's right, mister, probably not."

She huffed and puffed over the injustices of her life for half a block.

"My boss started his business as a penny arcade," Amy said, calmer now, "and blundered into selling polish sausages, which turned into a goldmine. He's very religious. Hard to find God on The Block, but my boss did it." She smiled at Tooey. "His family are sweet people. I just get mad."

"They sell good sandwiches if nothing else. What's it like working on The Block? It m-must be insane, huh?"

"It really is. I tell you, people are off their rockers. Drunk old ladies with their boobs hanging out. Boys dressed as girls going into an alley and not coming out for hours. Policemen in uniform peeing on the pavement."

That accent. "Payment?"

"You know, sidewalk."

"Why…do you put up with it?"

"What else am I going to do? Work for my father?"

"What's he do?"

"Owns a diner."

"Hunh," Tooey said with as much sarcasm as he could muster. "I can see why you wouldn't want to do that."

Amy laughed with a snort, and punched him lightly on the arm. "What about you?"

"I'm a waterman."

"Like a fisherman?"

"Yep."

"How do you know Heav… Dee?"

"We went to school together. Her father asked me to come get her."

"He just pull your name out of a hat?"

"I… I think so."

"She's not your girlfriend or anything?" Amy grinned at Tooey.

"No, no, no way. Dee's a nice girl, but…"

"Of course she is. That's why she's a stripper."

Tooey chuckled, thought to return her tender arm jab but resisted.

In the parking lot, Amy pointed to a lemon-yellow AMC Gremlin with a smudge-black racing stripe. She unlocked the driver's side door, and rolled down the window before turning to lean against her hatch-back and face Tooey. Assless by design, Amy's ride was one rank up from a go-cart, an off-the-line subcompact target for ridicule.

"Nice car?" He didn't mean to sound so skeptical.

"Hey! You down there in Yokelsville probably start driving your daddy's tractor when you're two, so you don't know it's a big deal for me to have my own vehicle. I'm the only girl I know my age with a driver's license. Only one of my boy friends has a license, and he doesn't have a car. Bawlmer kids don't drive."

"You have boyfriends?"

"Not that way. Boy. Friends."

Tooey liked the way Amy tried to stare him down.

"Can, can I have your phone number? I've got to find Dee and get her back to the Shore, but I'd like, I'd like to …uhm…call you sometime."

Amy had a pen handy. She wrote her number on a Gino's fast-food receipt. Tooey folded and tucked the paper in the back pocket of his jeans. He felt a familiar surge of red-faced bashfulness, but was able to pull back the throttle. "So you did see Dee today?"

"Oh yeah, sorry. She came in right before lunch."

"Good. She say where she was going? Where she'd be this afternoon?"

Amy grimaced. "She didn't, she told me to tell you to meet her at the Halfway Bar at nine."

"Tonight?"

"That's better than nine tomorrow morning, right?"

"Damn." Tooey looked at his watch. It was almost one and lavender.

Amy, out of nowhere, kissed Tooey right on his lips. It wasn't much more than a peck, but still. "Sorry," she blurted. "I've got to go," She jumped into her clunker, and slammed the door. The engine turned a couple times, and when it sounded like it was going to give up, caught and started with an accelerated roar. She said, "Sometimes you got to give it a little gas."

"You need a mechanic."

"Can you fix cars?"

"Sometimes."

"Huh. I might need someone more often than just sometimes." She put the car in reverse and Tooey stepped aside.

"Call me," Amy said.

"Drive careful."

"I always drive slow until I don't," Amy said before she peeled out of the parking lot, spraying gravel in her wake.

CHAPTER 20

Amy didn't mean to do that. She hoped Tooey wouldn't think she was a kook, but why wouldn't he? First of all she'd been rattling on like a Spring Grove escapee, and then she kissed him, and then she drove off like Mario Andretti.

And she should have asked him to the neighborhood block party. Her father wouldn't have liked it, but so what? Tooey was standing there looking at his watch, telling her he had nothing to do, and she didn't ask. Sometimes Amy got so caught up, so darned mouthy, she overlooked things. Amy strived to be more serious, more of a linear thinker, but she was born with, and aimed to keep, her artistic ways. She wondered if it was even possible to cultivate two such separate sides of a person's personality. That was one of the things Amy planned on learning in art school if she ever got there.

And of course he'd think she was a kook, everybody else seemed to.

But he did ask for her phone number.

Amy was almost more nervous that he would use it than not.

Arrrggghhh. The morning was a mess. The call from her boss. The argument with her mother about her sister's dress. Why couldn't her mother take Carol Lynn to Hochschild's? Plus baking cupcakes? It wasn't fair.

And work. What a pain. Without the promise of art school, which under the bright sunlight of July looked less and less likely, Amy was fearful that her current life would be the one she'd end up always living. She wasn't even supposed to be there today, she'd worked an extra day last week to make that happen. It was supposed to be her day off.

But.

If she hadn't gotten called in she might not have seen Tooey again.

When he came in today there was something different. He was still mellow, hesitant, cute in a country bumpkin sort of way, but this time more confident. Not that cocky chest-first kind of swagger she hated. Very different from the obsessed-with-cool boys Amy knew. She gave him her phone number, he was grinning like a dork. Amy was out of her uncle's parking lot and halfway down the street, and Tooey still hadn't stopped waving. No cool there.

Amy decided Tooey would call, and that if he asked she would go out with him. Her father would be mad. Amy was certain Tooey was older than she, maybe by a lot. Her dad might not like her so much these days, Amy thought, but he loved her and was protective. He was also lucky none of those mean and empty-headed neighborhood delinquents interested her anymore.

Strapping is what Grandmother Ruari would have called Tooey. His hands were rough. Being a fisherman must be hard work. His eyes changed color. Yesterday they were brownish, today bottle green and smoky. He had a determined jaw line.

So what would he ever see in her? Amy inspected herself in the rearview and almost ran a light. The hellish red hair. Sour milk skin. Freckles like splattered paint. High set ears and a billboard forehead. Bugs Bunny front teeth.

For lord's sake, he'd heard her snorty laugh, and saw her in her Herman Munster work boots.

The light turned green and Amy readjusted both her mirror and herself. What was it with this boy, this Tooey, who had her feeling loonier and more flummoxed than usual?

"Darn." She'd told Tooey what Dee had said, when and where to meet, but forgot to mention the whopping lunk who had come by work yesterday after Tooey left; when Keith called her back to help Debbie at the counter. Looking more dumb than dangerous, that squinchy-faced bruiser had also asked about Dee.

Amy considered returning to The Block to search for Tooey and inform him of her other visitor, but she decided her to-do list was full enough without doubling back.

Besides, this stranger she had such impulsive hots for, this fishmonger somehow involved with a stripper, was probably nothing but a dud, no more a part of her future than art school appeared to be, and not worth her effort.

"And," Amy asked herself, "what kind of stupid name is Tooey anyway?"

CHAPTER 21

Clacker Herbertson could not believe he lost Tooey that fast. Without even leaving the Eastern Shore, he'd once again proven himself a screw-up. Clacker sucked at his Tastee Freeze milkshake and aimed Blue Lightning toward the Chesapeake Bay.

Clacker was as tired of failure as he was of being broke. He believed he deserved better than the minimum wage donkeywork his father and brother counted on wringing out of him. Coming through for Mr. Bradnox was Clacker's escape plan. All the other errands and chores were warm-ups. This job was the real deal. Clacker could tell.

Not starting well deflated his spirits.

Contrary to any momentary doubts regarding his own capabilities, Clacker never possessed anything but staunch confidence in his El Camino. There wasn't much on the road she couldn't catch. As he drove through the tollgates on the western side of the Bay Bridge, visions of Tooey's rattling rust bucket took the edge off Clacker's anxiety.

The red, white, and blue Bicentennial decorations along Ritchie Highway made Clacker feel better, too. Being American was the greatest. Clacker's favorite movies were John Wayne war pictures. Clacker liked to fantasize that he'd have made a good soldier, maybe even a green beret, but had to admit he was relieved the draft ended before he'd been required to register. He had no interest in dying in some foreign jungle, but if called, Clacker would have answered. He was the most patriotic young person he knew.

Clacker hated how everybody his age disrespected the country, the law, the president. He liked things the way they were supposed to be. Screw all that longhair dope smoking hippie bullshit. It wasn't for him and never would be.

Thinking about how out of step he felt with the people he grew up with, Clacker went from angry to glum quicker than it took Blue Lightning to hit seventy.

Clacker had one girlfriend in high school, junior year, a girl from up-county named Kim. Kim stubbed out a cigarette in the funnel cake he bought her, and banged Fritzey Grimes behind Clacker's back. Clacker hadn't bothered with a girlfriend since. His dream girls were Angie Dickinson and Raquel Welch.

He never liked Dee Bradnox much. She'd always been stuck-up, and then turned into a piddling whore. Clacker couldn't figure how somebody could go around sucking random dicks all over the place while looking down their nose at people at the same time.

Dee was sexy though. He'd give her that. The way Clacker remembered, she had long blonde hair, a killer body, and a playful smirk offset by you-can't-handle-me eyes. She could make her voice sound like velvet and sandpaper at the same time.

But what an embarrassment to her family she turned out to be. Always running away, getting arrested, doing drugs. Never grateful, Dee had probably cost her parents a fortune. If Clacker had been born to such good luck, he'd have known how to honor and bolster his family's reputation. If Harris Bradnox had been his father instead of Bennett Herbertson Sr., things would have been a whole lot different. Of that Clacker was certain.

✦

"You Amy?" Clacker asked, standing in front of her, being the tough guy.

"I am," said Amy, looking anxious to get away from him and out the door.

"You know where Dee Bradnox is?"

She hairy-eyeballed him. Clacker didn't care for it a bit.

"Sure don't," Amy said without inflection.

"So you don't know where she is?"

"I don't know her."

"You don't know her," Clacker reiterated through crumpled twitches.

"I just said that," she sighed. "Sorry I can't help. Good luck finding your friend."

Clacker blocked her like a wall. "I didn't say she was my friend." He gave Amy the once over. "Your name is Amy and you don't know where I can find Dee Bradnox?"

"Hey, Hoss Cartwright, you're starting to freak me out, so I've got to ask you to step aside. I don't know your friend. I should have gotten off work hours ago and I'm out of patience. Now do I have to get that cop's attention," she tilted her head and cut her eyes at the patrolman having a dinner break, "or are we going to say good night?"

Clacker wasn't convinced, but he was confounded, so he stepped aside and let her pass. Feisty little redhead. Whatever was cooking back behind the counter sure smelled good. Clacker got in line to place an order.

✦

Late Friday night. Clacker thought he'd love The Block. He didn't at all.

Degenerates roamed the streets. Hawkers stood guard outside neon dungeons like the devil's gatekeepers. The skanky strippers onstage made the diseased bargirls look good. It was so humid that the polyester pants of Clacker's lime green leisure suit had shrunk, and were riding him in the crotch like a harness. Too many places he went smelled like pee.

Clacker entered a Swedish Erotica store. Row after row of nudie magazines and 8mm films were offered for sale. Titles ranged from glamour girl stuff to activities so hardcore, Clacker had never imagined them possible, much less desirable. There was a smattering of soft, romantic type movies, the name Emmanuelle prevalent on the packaging, but there were far more numerous S&M offerings. There were even copies of what was purported to be a snuff movie with a handwritten sign exclaiming 'Banned in Baltimore!' Perverts packed the aisles.

Toward the back of the store was a row of movie stalls that men entered and exited like voting booths. Clacker paid a buck's worth of quarters to see what Linda Lovelace was, in fact, up to. He saw. She lost all appeal. He'd watched stag films at the firehouse and the Pythias hall, but never anything like this. Even the small amount of actual sex Clacker had experienced in his life was less graphic than what he saw onscreen. A reel started with Marilyn Chambers and a black man. Clacker left the booth repulsed, the movie playing behind him.

Making his way back through the maze of peep shows, Clacker witnessed two men go into a stall together. He was almost to the staircase when a door swung open and some old man tumbled out ass-backwards with his drawers down around his dress shoes. He banged his head against the wall on the opposite side of the hallway, and flopped to the floor. Clacker had to step over him to get away.

Clacker Herbertson searched The Block another couple hours. He got to see the aftermath of a bar fight that had spilled out onto the street, some dudes were in handcuffs on the sidewalk, but at midnight, he drove Blue Lightning down to the city-owned parking lot alongside the police station, where he thought he might be safe from the ruins of civilization, and went to sleep in his car.

CHAPTER 22

N**obody ever gave** Tooey a kiss that made queasy feel good before. He shook it off.

Tooey started Saturday with two missions, #1 Get Dee and #2 Get home, but both objectives had hinged on good news from Amy. Amy told him Dee said to meet at nine, and Tooey's plans deflated like one of his truck's raggedy-to-a-hazard tires. Now he saw how pin-holed his shabby strategy had been all along.

Walking back to his truck, Tooey noticed a theater marquee with an afternoon showing of *One Flew Over the Cuckoo's Nest* beginning soon. He knew how soon by checking his watch, the watch that told him time, but also that he was restless and anxious. His ring agreed, but thought maybe he was also a bit more content than that.

He watched *Cuckoo's Nest* again. Tooey thought that if he could watch movies like that anytime he wanted he'd never get anything else done. It was just so good. So sad and funny and true. Tooey knew he'd die believing Jack Nicholson was, in that movie, as great as an actor could ever be; and Nurse Ratched was scarier than the *Jaws* shark and that creepy *Omen* kid put together.

Tooey never understood why people disliked going to theaters alone. He did whenever there was something he wanted to see. His grandmother was a film fan, but her tastes and Tooey's didn't often align. Moviestar rarely cared to attend. On occasion, Tooey would hit the drive-in with a group of watermen and their girlfriends and wives, but those excursions were more about partying than movie-going, and at best, the atmosphere was distracting. In the worst circumstances a fight or a messy break-up would ruin the fun, and twice, someone had set something on fire.

Sometimes alone was the best way to do things a person enjoyed.

Though it would be nice to see a movie with Amy sometime.

Something funny.

Or romantic maybe.

⚓

Tooey went to his room. He didn't see Willy Nelson. Willy Nelson's chair sat empty on the balcony walkway. Tooey lay down on his moonscape mattress, watched wrestling, and fell asleep while reading his magazines.

He woke up and it was almost eight thirty.

His truck wouldn't start. Wouldn't even crank. Tooey popped the hood and poked around, but after investigating obvious causes, he was frazzled, at a loss. He'd kick his own ass, but didn't have time. Right now getting his hands on Delores Goddamn Bradnox was his focus. There was no way he was missing Dee. They'd have to come back for the truck. He went into the motor court's office and asked the listless desk clerk how to find a taxi. The clerk handed him a business card and pointed at the wall-mounted pay phone.

⚓

The Halfway was one of The Block's neighborhood bars. There were no dancers or hawkers, no bar girls or deejays. It was dark inside. Tooey felt like he'd walked into a 1970's version of a Humphrey

Bogart movie. There were enormous hats, bow ties, and wide lapels, painted-on shadows, and an assemblage of Peter Lorres. Rick was a mobster, Isla a stripper on break. Sam the piano player would have been told to shut the fuck up and let time go by without the accompaniment.

Dee Bradnox sat in a booth in the back with a straight-on view of the door. Tooey approached and saw that a bulb was missing from the wall fixture behind her. All the other velvet-backed booths were bathed in a cheap red candelabra glow. Dee pretended to be surprised to see him. Her performance didn't play well.

"Tooey Walter. What brings you here?" Dee wore a curly brown wig and a badly crocheted skull cap. A half-finished cocktail kept her company. "I'm just kidding," she said. "Lighten up, honey. Sit with me. You want something?"

"Yep. I want you to come with me. I'm here to take, to take you home."

"I meant to drink."

"I know what you meant."

"You can't even say hi a minute? Come on, Tooey. How long's it been?"

"Long time, Dee. How you been?"

She laughed and patted the seat next to her. Tooey sat down.

"Have a drink with me."

"No thanks. Where'd you run off to?"

"A co-worker's place. She's raising her son by herself. You'd be surprised how many women do that. She's amazing. Going to school, too. Dances to keep food on the table and the tuition paid. We keep our friendship off the radar. Like with Amy at Polish Jack's, it helps to have friends nobody else knows about." She took a drink. "And you know me, never too hot at holding on to friends."

"Come on. Let's go."

"You were always nice to me though." There was no emotion in her statement.

"What the hell was that in the bar last night?" Tooey demanded to know. "Did you know your father was sending some, somebody for you? Why go all James Bond? Why didn't you just tell us where you were?"

"I wasn't ready for pick-up."

"You better be ready now."

"I am. Almost."

"Uh-uh. Bottoms up. Let's hit the road." He tapped the side of her glass.

"We have to go back to my apartment."

"You can drop that back of the throat whisper of yours, Dee. It don't, it don't do nothing for me. I say we go and we go now and the hell with your apartment."

Dee withered Tooey's resolve with a scalding look that told him things would go easier if he just complied with her commands.

He said, "Wh-where is your apartment and why do we have to go there?"

"It's close enough. We have to go get the case."

"Did you start that free-for-all so you could snatch that man's case?"

"It's my case."

"It's your case?"

"It is now."

"So you set off a riot, stole, stole, stole a man's belongings, and hid out for almost twenty four hours, letting me cool my heels?"

"His name is Salt. I didn't know where you were. I figured you'd stop in Polish Jack's at some point, so I went to see Amy at work and—"

"Well, you're lucky, because she wasn't even supposed to be there today."

"—and figured if I told you to meet me tonight you'd be more likely get the message." She finished her drink in two gulps. "And go back to my apartment with me."

"Why? That man whose case you ripped off going to whup your ass to get it back? You trying to get me whupped too, Dee? I want to know what's up before I take one step in any direction. 'Cause I'll tell you, right now my com-, my compass points southeast."

"I can't go home without that case."

"Sure you can."

"I can't." She stared at Tooey with a familiar defiance. "I've been through a lot with Salt, Tooey. You don't know what my life is. Now he wants to kill me."

"All the more reason to get out of Dodge. You think I want to go somewhere somebody like that might be waiting for me? I swear Dee, you're the same exact spoiled kid you've always been. You oughta be ashamed of yourself. We should go get my truck and drive across that bay and go the hell home."

"I'm not leaving without the case."

"Your daddy would want…"

Dee gave him that look again and Tooey didn't bother finishing. He sat there chewing the inside of his jaw.

"You crochet that hat yourself?" Tooey finally spoke up.

She beamed with pride. Tooey stood and said, "Well, you oughta juh-just stick with getting naked. Heaven."

Chapter 23

When Salt Wade was a boy, he'd hide under the house from his mama. He'd find a soft dark place to hunker down with his Silvertone transistor radio, turn the volume way low and listen to the colored stations. Sonny Boy, Little Walter, Muddy and the rest touched Salt's soul, but Howlin' Lobo brought messages from an angry God. That voice, the way the Lobo played the harp, so sweet, so pitiful, yet demonic and capable of ferocious violence. Salt Wade loved the Blues, but worshipped Howlin' Lobo most of all.

Howlin' Lobo's voice was all that ever made Salt Wade cry.

Salt never sang, never learned to play. He clung to the mysterious joy music brought him. "Knowing something ain't the same as believing in it," Salt would say. And Salt believed in the Blues, believed in the music's brutal truths. He believed it when the music told him no one could be trusted.

Heaven stole his case to prove it. This woman, not much more than a girl, took advantage. Doing that to Salt Wade required a rare gift. Salt had started feeling protective, looking out for her against his instincts. Heaven was feisty, able to say what she thought with her lopsided grin alleviating the most cutting remark. That smile and those eyes were weapons he'd come to learn she used, along with the rest of her arsenal, to try and make everything always work her way.

But Salt Wade was no pushover. Heaven might have thought she had him wrapped around her fuck-finger, but Salt knew better. He had affection for her, there was no doubt to that, but he would kill the bitch to get his case back.

⅄

Salt's kin Georgie, a degenerate gambler, worked in an Illinois veteran's hospital. Because Georgie didn't want his new bride to know he lost their nest egg in a basement poker game, Georgie had borrowed more than he should have from cousin Salt. Georgie swore he'd pay Salt back, but a year was past, and Georgie had quit checking in.

Salt was ready to write the loan off, put a boot in Georgie's ass next time he saw him. Then he got the call.

"Oh, shit, Salt. You are going to freak out what I got my hands on," Georgie said. Salt could tell Georgie was both excited and spooked. Georgie told Salt of the metal cigar box with the trick lock, and how he'd stolen it.

Salt said, "If it's what you say it is, cuz, if it don't clear your tab, it'll put a hell-all dent in it."

"That's what I was hoping. I got a couple days coming," Georgie whispered. "Debra thinks I got training in D.C. I'm gonna come see you instead, cool?"

"Deliver me that treasure soon as you can, boy."

Salt Wade wiped Georgie Wade's slate clean upon receipt.

⅄

Friday night, Salt had snorted two slender lines before heading out to check on Heaven at Nick's Mousetrap. The coke was decent enough, he could feel that drip in his sinuses, but some better stuff had come in.

He was scheduled to meet with Little Mervin's boys on Saturday and get straight with them, pick up his share of this fresh batch his connections were anticipating.

Heroin was Baltimore's big street seller, but Salt did not care to be much involved with that. Of course, he moved an ounce or two here or there, but cocaine was Salt's drug of choice and his primary income producer. His humble stable of whores performed much better jacked up on Peruvian marching powder than smack, and Salt had aspirations. Coke was where the money people spent their rolled-up dollar bills.

The Block was busy. Players and rubes alike clogged the sidewalks, and with the win at Memorial Stadium, all the drunken O's fans had landed like an invading army of easy marks. Salt anticipated a profitable weekend.

The coke had him arrogant with confidence. Salt carried the case, couldn't bear to be without it, but couldn't conceive of anybody nuts enough to try to separate him from it.

Heaven was at the top of his evening's agenda, but Salt took care of other business on his way. He made sure his chicks were in place, stopped by to see his most useful bartender friends. Spoke to the cop on the corner for a moment, and said hey to the Jewish-Mexican hawker, Levi.

Salt pimp-walked into Nick's Mousetrap slapping a twenty in the doorman's palm, and pulling his trigger finger at the smiling barman. The place was rocking, the long narrow room jammed with people. Salt could see Heaven working it, up on some guy back there like an Old Testament Jezebel. Good girl. Salt recognized the guy as a plainclothes cop, but before he could recall a name, the narc reared back and slapped Heaven hard enough to spin her. Undercover cop or not, Salt knew that motherfucker had to pay.

Salt launched, landed, and started swinging all in the same fraction of an eye blink. Both men went down, with Salt on top, but his dominance was temporary. The narc bucked and wiggled, a rubber room madman, and Salt's best-aimed punches didn't connect to much more than elbows and wrists. Salt couldn't even land a good one using his metal case. Someone's fist, an asteroid from outer space, sent Salt flying sideways into the mob, enabling Heaven to steal his case from him. She tried to break his fingers doing it, too.

If he'd caught her eye, Salt bet Heaven would have cut her shit without hesitation, but she would not look him in the face. Not until the case was loose. Then she stared right at Salt, smiled, and stuck her tongue out at him. Salt wanted to pull it out by the roots.

A desire hampered by the snapping of handcuffs.

Salt knelt among the sidewalk throng outside Nick's with the other disturbers of the peace, none of them the narcs that he saw start the whole shebang. These other dummies lined up next to Salt had all been too slow or too drunk to get their licks in and get out before getting busted. If somebody hadn't slapped the bracelets on him in the blurry moments after Heaven disappeared, they certainly would never have had Salt Wade out there on the concrete like a common chump.

The on-duty beat cop walked behind Salt and leaned over, checking the handcuffs, putting on a show. "Hang in there a few minutes," was all he said.

Salt smiled. Buying a guy a cup of coffee now and again can go a long way.

ㅅ

Born Baptist, raised crazy, Salt Wade considered himself to be a God-fearing heathen.

Salt saw his daddy once. His mother Carla was an evangelical maniac with an angel's singing voice. Carla Taylor, of the bootlegging Arkansas Taylors, abused her bastard child in religion's name out of habit. She used to claim the boy had a devil inside, and refused to see or speak to the man he'd become. Give Carla credit for consistency though, she had no more to do with the rest of her petty clan than she did with her son.

Carla pushed him out her door on his twelfth birthday. He lived on a neighbor's farm until he could no longer suffer the beatings and forced labor. After that, he bunked with various relatives, friends, or strangers, off and on, here and there, across the south, including Uncle Toot who worked at the notorious Tucker State Prison Farm and Uncle Licky Bird, the family hatchet man. Toot's wife, Aunt Girl, was first to call the boy 'Salt'. At Licky Bird's, Salt slept on a pool table for two years.

⅄

The beat cop uncuffed Salt and told him that the undercover narcs had all scattered with no desire to pursue any charges. Salt hit a few of Heaven's favorite haunts, all lost causes. He drove to her one room apartment above the liquor store, let himself in with a key he'd had made, and ransacked the joint. He flipped the sparse furniture and kicked holes in the walls. He felt like he should explode the place, but snorted a fat line instead. The phone rang before he got the chance to decide how to proceed.

"Hello. Rotten cooter's residence."

There was no response from the other end.

"You bring me my property right here right now," Salt said, "and I won't touch you. I'll give you twenty minutes to get here, after that we'll see. You make me come look for you, Heaven, and things are gonna end bad.

"See, you make fun of my upbringing, but up in them hills, you learn things. I got this one uncle'll blow your head off. Tie you up, stick a pair of M-80s in your nostrils. How about the Judas chair? You ever hear of that? That'd be a good one for you, you dirty thieving slit. Set you down on top a cone of sheet metal over a campfire. Cleave you in half. Sound fun? You're going to find out if you don't bring me my case in the next twenty minutes."

The line clicked dead. Salt waited half an hour. On his way out he resisted the urge to turn on the gas oven, and watch from down the street as the whole corner went ka-boom.

Instead, he paced the city's streets until well past dawn.

Until he fizzled out.

$$\blacktriangle$$

Salt awoke Saturday evening, showered, put on his denim jumpsuit and his Dingo cowboy boots. Not tall, Salt preferred platform shoes, but tonight his shit-kickers would see duty.

After a couple bumps of coke, Salt filled a pinkie-finger sized vial from his private hidden stash, turned off his expensive customized stereo, and locked his apartment door behind him. The corridor smelled dank, half-drowned. Reminded Salt of Key West.

A few years before, Salt had made his way down to the very tip of America's dong. A guy he knew from one lockup or another scored him a gig at a plush resort brimming with reward and promise. Salt made friends, dated a concierge named Liz, and was well liked by his employers until they caught him stealing out of their guests' suitcases. He did nine months at Glades Correctional and traveled north after his release.

Within weeks, Salt was in Baltimore working as a runner for Little Mervin Wallace, the city's drug kingpin. When Mervin was sentenced to a hard fifteen for conspiracy to distribute heroin last year, Salt Wade decided it was time for him to scale his way up the ladder of crime. Baltimore was the Wild, Wild West when nobody was in command.

Chapter 24

"**What's your matter**, Salty?" asked the black man holding a bowl of spices he'd hand mixed himself. "You don't groove on seafood?"

They sat on opposite sides of a picnic table covered with brown-paper in the back office of a downtown restaurant. There was a pile of steamed crabs between them.

"I don't eat nothing I can't see where it lives," Salt said. "But glad you could get me in early tonight though. Thanks."

The black man, Clyde, cracked a claw on the edge of the table. He dipped the claw into his seasoning. "You see where every hamburger, every drumstick, every pork chop you eat called home?"

"I see cows, chickens, and pigs in fields, barns, and sties," Salt said. "I don't know what the fuck is going on under that ocean."

Clyde laughed. Salt didn't.

⋏

Salt Wade had rejected the straight life Florida once offered. An outlaw was what he was born to be. He'd started doing his homework, putting together the pieces of Baltimore's crime puzzle as soon as he hit town. Figured if he was going to be a criminal, might as well shoot for the top, pun intended, and not a bad one at that, Salt reckoned. He even said it out loud once in a while; thought of it as the motto on his coat of arms. The Lord Cornwall ran Baltimore vice for decades. Connected to the New York families, he vanished while facing federal charges. Depending on who was doing the talking, Cornwall either fled while on appeal, or escaped from prison hiding in the undercarriage of a transport bus, or maybe inside a laundry barrel. He high-tailed it to either Cuba, Canada, or Israel. Salt figured the way the real mafia worked, the most probable end for the esteemed Lord Cornwall was sporting a pair of concrete kicks at the bottom of the city's filthy harbor.

The specifics were inconsequential to Salt. There were lessons to learn. The Lord's absence destabilized The Block until Little Mervin Wallace, Cornwall's protégé and successor, rose to the top of the city's crime heap with his ability to squelch bloodshed and his aspirations of becoming "the world's best drug dealer." Good guys and bad guys alike would testify Mervin Wallace had far exceeded his goal. Mervin's power was absolute. It was said that during the '68 riots, the Baltimore establishment reached out through back channels for Little Mervin's help in settling the frenzied neighborhoods. Little Mervin was the one who shut that revolution down. Anarchy's bad for business.

With the help of a network of lowlifes that included both Salt Wade and Clyde above him, Little Mervin moved fifty kilos of heroin a month at $70,000 per, and was working his way toward those numbers with coke. Mervin oversaw the city's drugs, gambling, loan sharking, protection rackets, and prostitution. For Mervin Wallace, it was a good time to be a gangster.

Until he caught that hard fifteen, and once again B-more chaos ruled.

Salt took that as a sign maybe it was his time to rise.

Salt said, "I ain't taking less, Clyde."

"You will if you want to get your hands on some of this," Clyde told him. "Dorsal, give Mr. Salty here a taste of what we just got in."

The monster to Clyde's left pulled a baggie and a third of a soda straw from inside his dungaree jacket. The even bigger guy to Clyde's right did nothing but sit there. Clyde kept eating crabs, rummaging inside the shell for that primal mustard that agitated Salt's gag reflex.

Salt hit both nostrils. He dabbed into the bag with a finger and rubbed ten bucks worth across his gums. A circus opened for business in his head.

"Thing is," Clyde said, "even though Mervin's running things from inside, we the ones out here working it. We honor him; Mervin's still boss, so we can't take from his end. But this ain't getting it. You want in from now on; we got to rearrange your payment plan. We taking an extra ten percent off the top."

"We?"

Clyde, smug, looked up from his feast and said, "Me. How 'bout that then?"

"I ain't ta—" Salt's sinuses were so numb he couldn't finish his declaration.

"Charge more on your end, lessen your hurt. Or don't. You can pay right now what you into us for, shake hands, and walk away, we alright." Clyde sucked the meat out of a crab crevice. "But you know you can't be doing no business in my city."

"I thought it was Mervin's city."

"I was born and raised here, too, white boy. Just like Mervin. It's our city."

Salt held his arms out, palms skyward. He scanned the room. "Ours?"

"Mervin's and mine's. And Dorsal's. But not Joe's." Clyde looked to the mountain of muscle to his right. "Never Joe's. Joe like you. He ain't from here."

Salt returned Dorsal's coke. Clyde sneered and gave a faint nod. Dorsal pulled a quarter pound brick from a gym bag under the table, wrapped it from the roll of brown paper mounted on the wall, and held it out for Salt to take.

Clyde said, "I don't got to tell you, Saltine, you into us for quite a bit. I'm starting to think you might be sniffing more than you selling lately. You might want to get a handle on that. This shit make you delusional you let it."

Salt bit his lip.

"Go ahead and take this, see how you do," Clyde said. "Maybe not dip into it too much and don't worry too much about your profit this time. You be loyal, hardworking, yours'll come. And I've taken a shine to you, Salty Dog, you's like our city, y'know. Bit southern, bit northern." Clyde took a break from picking crabs, put his elbows on the table, and held his hands in the air, a surgeon. "This your chance to get on a level playing field again with Mervin and us. You move those 113 grams in the next few days, say Wednesday, bring us your regular plus that extra, build that trust, brother, and we see about setting you up with a nice hefty batch next time."

"Wednesday?" Salt never had to meet that stiff a turn-around before.

"Holiday weekend – business oughta be slamming. Let's move it to Tuesday. Call and ask for Dorsal to schedule an appointment." He dismissed Salt with a wave. Big Joe shifted in his seat.

Salt was starting toward the exit with his marching orders and his ego pinched when Clyde hollered to him, "Hey Saltlick, Dorsal wants to know where that funky case at you been carrying?"

"I don't know yet," said Salt Wade, "but I intend to find out. Thank you for asking, Dorsal. You got good etiquette. A regular goddamn Emily Post."

⁂

Salt went back home to break down his dope and make a few calls. Clyde's coke was maybe the finest Salt had ever tasted. He packaged a few eightballs and grams, and refilled his personal vial with the new high quality stuff. Checking in with a cadre of contacts on the telephone, he hit the jackpot with a night manager at The Halfway Bar.

When Salt arrived, Heaven was leaving the Halfway with some gangling kid. Salt followed them through the congested streets without Heaven spotting him when she glanced back. At one of the murkier corners, his prey darted down a side street. Salt picked up his pace but made sure to stay out of sight. They stopped once, argued, moved on; Salt not needing to hear to know that Heaven had gotten her way. Nearing a construction site, Heaven and the kid edged along a tall wooden alleyway fence and there, in shadows so deep even werewolves would get the willies, Salt made his move.

Chapter 25

The night before, when Salt had answered the phone at her place, Dee was not surprised. She had expected he'd go there first.

Dee made the call from Orchid's apartment. She sat silent, listening to Salt curse and threaten her for a minute before she hung up.

Orchid and her baby called it a night. Dee lay on the couch and made an effort to get some sleep. The adrenaline coursing through her body, combined with her scheming thoughts, would not allow it. An hour or so before dawn, she threw off the lightweight cover that Orchid had provided her, and tiptoed to her co-worker's bedroom door. She peeked in and saw that the baby was stirring in its thrift store crib. Orchid slept nearby on a twin-sized Murphy bed.

Dee picked up Orchid's son, and went back to the couch.

With the infant on her chest, Dee watched the boy gurgle and smile, watched him twist and struggle to take in, to understand, the world around him. The baby reached out and touched Dee's face. It took all of Dee's willpower not to weep.

They nodded off, the child's dainty fingers wrapped around one of her own.

▲

Orchid woke up late that Saturday morning. She was appreciative of the extra sack time. After feeding her son, and tucking him back in, the two women drank coffee and talked about Dee's dilemma.

Wearing borrowed street clothes, a brunette wig, the hat she had crocheted herself, and carrying an over-sized suede handbag of Orchid's, Dee first stopped at Polish Jack's to talk to Amy. When she returned to her own building, Mr. Toy, the man who ran the first floor liquor store there, swore to God he hadn't seen Salt. Dee asked if he was sure, and looked for signs of lying before going upstairs to her third-story, top-floor rat hole.

Everything was trashed – her microscopic living space was even more depressing than usual. She noted the severed phone cord, and worried for a moment that Salt might be inside the apartment with her, but there were so few places to hide, Dee checked them all in a glance.

Dee kept the bag holding the case in sight while she showered. She considered ditching Tooey Walter and leaving town on her own. The bus station wasn't an option. Salt would have that covered. His whores would be watching. A cab would work. It'd be expensive, but who cared. Tooey would make his own way to the Eastern Shore sooner or later.

Salt had ripped and shredded most of Dee's clothes before leaving them strewn all over the floor in piles. Finding a salvageable pair of jeans and a blouse, Dee was concerned that Tooey might cross paths with Salt if they were both out on The Block looking for her. She prayed Tooey would get her message and lay low until nine. Dee knew Salt met with Clyde at nine on Saturday nights.

If there had been anyone there to suggest she should make sure Tooey was safe instead of taking the case and splitting, Dee would have defied their advice with practiced habit and, in her own best interest, been home hours ago. Despite her instincts, however, Dee felt protective of Tooey and did not want the worst that could happen to happen to him. She felt responsible. It didn't come natural.

Dee locked her apartment's flimsy door with the first of two keys on her troll doll key ring. She stepped across and down the hall to a disabled hallway dumbwaiter, and with the second key removed the padlock from what she'd come to think of as her safety deposit box. Extracting Salt's cherished case from Orchid's tote, Dee placed it next to a modest bundle of cash and a jewelry box that were already inside the otherwise-obsolete aluminum square.

She went back to Orchid's.

Went back to wait until she could meet with Tooey and go home.

$$\blacktriangle$$

Now, leaving the Halfway Bar with Tooey in tow, Dee set a brisk pace through The Block's Saturday night crowds. She said, "Come on, dude, pick it up. Where's your car?"

Tooey told her it was a truck, where he'd left it, and why. She wanted to punch him in his stupid country face.

"Broke down? Are you kidding me, Tooey? You come to get me in a broken down crab truck?" She looked to see if anyone followed. "We should get a taxi. I don't like being on the street too long."

"Great," Tooey said. "Let's go back. Call a taxi."

"No," Dee said, "come on. We'll walk. I know short cuts and my place isn't all that far. We'll get a cab to your truck. You can get your truck running, right?"

"Yeah. I, I guess. I think so. If not, I'll make arrangements."

"Weren't you a Boy Scout? That 'Be Prepared' thing never took, huh?"

Tooey stepped up, walked beside her, maybe a half step ahead despite not knowing where they were going. "Let's just go get this case and then back to my motel. And then back, back to the Shore."

"Ugh. You say "the Shore" like it's paradise."

"Compared to sneaking around this city wi-with you, fighting policemen in a riot you started so you could steal money from some dirtbag psycho who—"

"I never said there was money in the case."

"You know, that's right." Tooey stopped. "I'm not taking another step until you tell me what's in that case that's so valuable and important."

She surveyed their surroundings. "I don't know," she conceded, clasping him by his forearm and starting off again. "I can't get it open."

They came to a commercial building site, and Dee led him down a dark alleyway. A distant security light conjured shadows of undetermined depth.

Without knowing for sure how, Dee sensed someone behind them.

She turned to confront their pursuer, but her yelp was cut short. Salt clipped her across her throat with a karate chop. Her hands flew to her neck and her jaw unfastened like a hinge broke. Crashing to her knees, Dee saw Tooey rush Salt.

Salt sidestepped. As Tooey barreled past, Salt grabbed Tooey's collar and pulled that ugly-ass brown shirt right over Tooey's head. He clocked Tooey above the left ear, and whirled him in a circle. Tooey lost his footing, and as he pitched forward, Salt planted a helpful kick square in Tooey's back, firing him headfirst into the wooden construction fence so hard a board cracked. Tooey went down like Sweet Connie Hamzy.

Salt smiled at Dee. "Hey baby," he snarled. "Good to see you, you deceitful cooze. Ready to say adios?"

Before Dee could try to answer, she caught movement from the corner of her eye. A figure tore past her narrowing vision, bee-lining, and colliding into Salt like a tractor-trailer loaded with bricks. Dee felt as though she hadn't taken a breath in days. She wanted to pass out, keel over. The one and only thought keeping her conscious was, "What the hell is Clacker Herbertson doing here?"

CHAPTER 26

Clacker had awakened that Saturday morning in the driver's seat of his prized possession with a saturating dread weighing on him. The temperature was already 90 degrees and the air was soggy.

The city squeezed in. He needed to find Tooey or Dee, or at least what Dee owed her father, and get back to the Shore soon as he could. Clacker couldn't stand much more time spent anywhere near that Block. He made a sweep of the neighborhood and found it even more revolting in sunlight. It was sad and it was hot and nobody knew nothin' about no Dee Bradnox.

Clacker walked, aimless, up and down East Baltimore and the surrounding side streets, asking anybody that caught his eye and looked coherent about Dee.

At lunchtime, Clacker found a phone booth and called Mr. Bradnox collect. Damned guy acted like he wasn't going to accept until the operator got snippy.

"I lost Tooey," Clacker said into the dirty mouthpiece. "I can't find him or Dee. Nobody around here has ever even heard of her, and that Polock girl wasn't no help."

"How'd you lose Tooey?" Bradnox had a tone.

"I think he knew I was sticking him and he gave me the slip." Clacker's scalp itched. "Tooey always was pretty smart, now that I give it some thought."

"So what are you going to do? Give up?"

"No sir. I've put a few feelers out. I won't come back until I got Dee."

"And what she owes me."

Without thought, Clacker said, "It's money right?"

"You'll know it when you see it. Whatever it is, Dee will have it and she'll want to protect it."

Clacker waited for more direction.

"So I guess that's it?" Bradnox said. "You'll be back here soon with my daughter and those valuables?"

"Bing bang, Mr. Bradnox."

"Well, that's good then. I'll see you when you get here."

Clacker could hear Bradnox breathing into his phone like it was work. The older man said, "Well go ahead and hang up, Herbertson."

⅄

Because he didn't know what else to do, Clacker bought a bag of little hamburgers, and walked to the harbor. There were modern buildings under construction everywhere he looked. He got the sense this haggard waterfront was straining to become something different from what it was, but to him it still felt misshapen and haunted.

He sat down on a creaking bulkhead abutting a derelict pier, and gulped the first of a dozen sliders. He smelled hot tar. It reminded him of home

Clacker knew there'd be plenty work here for a guy like him. Nobody humped harder or picked up mechanical knowledge quicker. He had an eye for design and could do some complicated math in his head. He could relate to a world of steel and brick, wrought iron and glass.

Construction came easy, but no one ever listened when he spoke. They focused on his missing tooth, his tics, his sweaty forehead, and deemed him stupid. Clacker was never going to get any real chances. The Dee Bradnox's of the world got the breaks and wasted them. He chewed the remaining burgers with increasing anguish.

The skyline across the harbor provided scant charm. He saw all the shapes and angles, the sharp and shining office buildings in the foreground, surrounded by an original flagstone city. Church steeples looked like ships' masts.

He could see the Domino Sugar sign, the new Science Center; it looked off to him with those severe and jutting corners, and the Bromo-Seltzer Tower with its distinctive clock that instead of numbers, displayed letters spelling out the antacid's brand name.

Clacker sat there eating little hamburgers and smoking cigarettes, watching time pass and the world changing.

He distrusted his strength and his desire to keep up and do the same.

Swinging his feet over the edge of the retainer wall, Clacker didn't notice the sun had gone down until he saw a family of playful rats scurry out of a crack in the concrete bulkhead.

The sliders had been tasty. Clacker could have eaten a few more, but what he really had a taste for was soup. Crab soup, oyster stew, chicken noodle, it didn't matter. Clacker's mama made excellent soups. Clacker missed home.

It was a quarter to S, according to the Bromo-Seltzer clock. The crush of the city at dusk became so unbearable Clacker had to get moving.

⋏

Clacker finished another tour of The Block sidewalks. He couldn't bring himself to go inside anywhere. He'd resigned himself to defeat yet couldn't quit. He worried maybe he was doomed to walk these repulsive avenues forever. He could never go home without completing Mr. Bradnox's business. His search would never end.

Clacker slipped down a side street to find a place to urinate. As he emerged from behind an abandoned commercial building, two people came bopping down the boulevard, and like magic, there they were. He wouldn't have pegged Dee, but that was Tooey plain as vanilla pudding.

Clacker took a step back, and they walked right by.

He watched them hesitate at a construction alley, and that's when he noticed the man dogging their steps. Clacker let the stranger wearing the stupid jumpsuit pass. Clacker followed behind. Tooey and Dee turned down the alley. Their stalker gathered speed. Clacker did too. Reaching the alley, Clacker was flat-out running.

Tooey was laid out, Dee kneeling and daze-faced. The stranger was saying something to her as Clacker zeroed in. He stopped talking and turned his upper body in Clacker's direction. Clacker, at full speed, jammed both fists into the stranger's chest with enough force to rearrange every organ in there.

Even in the near lightless alley, Clacker could see Dee Bradnox looking at him like she always did, like he had cooties. Except now her stare was tinted with shock. Shock, and what Clacker thought might be teary-eyed gratitude.

Either that or she couldn't breathe.

The stranger with the queer clothes and the poofy hair squirmed on the ground. He tried to stand, floundered, and settled for uttering some lackluster threat. Clacker kicked him quiet.

CHAPTER 27

There was a fight to the death going on in Harris Bradnox's lower intestines. He had just gotten off the phone with the Herbertson kid.

Plodding around his bedroom after having spent the morning in his office, Harris couldn't figure what was wrong with his daughter's generation. No work ethic, no appreciation, a sense of entitlement Harris believed never existed before. All they knew was SEX, DRUGS, AND ROCK AND ROLL. Wore it right on their T-shirts. They believed in nothing, saw no use in even trying to make their mark. They hooted and hollered, over what nobody was ever quite certain, all the while being babied by mommy and daddy. His daughter the worst of them.

Then a Herbertson comes along who still believes in authority and hard work, and he's thicker than Type M mortar.

Because he felt so sick, Harris was avoiding most of the Bicentennial events. He needed to attend a flag raising at the yacht club at three, and the festivities at the VFW on Sunday. Harris hoped he could get through both without farting a rendition of *Shave and a Haircut* in front of an assembled crowd of patriotic celebrants.

He changed into what he thought of as his work uniform. Khakis and sport shirt, brown leather shoes and a fashionable tie some real estate agent had given him. Most times Harris couldn't care less about what he wore. In general, however, he believed his inexpensive duds helped him fit in with people he'd felt superior to all his life.

It was past noon. Annette and the dog were both still sound asleep under their covers. Even in slumber, Harris' wife was the classiest woman he ever saw.

Harris' bed was in an adjacent room that shared a walk-in closet. He hadn't slept there, or anywhere for that matter, for more than a couple hours at a time, for as many nights as he could remember. He was running on empty.

He was still in love with his wife, despite their growing distance. Annette had been sixteen and pregnant when she married twenty-four year old Harris Bradnox. Her parents were mortified and furious, but at least Harris was also from a respectable family. The wedding took place within weeks of Annette missing her period. Their little girl had been the bridge that connected them.

He turned off the closet light, and walked over to his office above the garage.

Talking to Herbertson reminded Harris of the call he'd received from his daughter the week before. After months of no communication, with Harris believing he and Annette might finally be free of the chaos and heartbreak Dee brought to their lives, she called. He told Dee that he and her mother were done with her, that whatever problems she had she'd have to take care of herself.

"We've written you off," is what he told her.

"I know. I'm begging you to let me come home."

"Why?"

"Because I need to come home, daddy. I need another chance."

"Do you know what you have cost us over the years, Delores? Your mother and me? Do you know the embarrassment you have caused us, the financial strain you've put on this family? I can't take it anymore. I can't allow you to come back here and start your crap again. The drugs, the drinking, the screwing around. You can't change what you've done, and now it's too late to change what you are."

Dee was quiet a moment. "I am guilty of a lot of things I can't make right. But daddy, I can pay you back."

"What do you mean by that?"

"I can pay you back," she said.

He hadn't heard from her since.

Sitting down at his desk, Harris glanced at the one framed picture of Dee he still kept within sight. She was twelve in the photo, his flawless daughter. Beautiful, charming, smart. His Delores dressed in Christmas Eve nightclothes and beaming like the child she was before things went so bad.

Knocked up at fourteen. The boy should have known better, and took a nice beating from one of Harris' contractors to ensure he would from then on, but looking back, that punk kid was as much a victim of the whole shameful episode as anybody. His fate was sealed as soon as Dee set her sights on him.

Harris arranged a quickie abortion with their family doctor. It was a miracle the small town everybody-knows-everybody rumor mill never got a good grip on what happened that spring. Those who knew kept their mouths shut.

Things were never the same, though. Harris couldn't even look his little girl in the eye anymore. And of course, before long, Dee was regular fodder for the gossips anyway, so the abortion was just the beginning of the soul-wringing Dee had inflicted upon him.

But now Harris's financial ship had run aground, and his wayward daughter, of all people, might be able to buy him some time. Eastern Shore real estate development was on the cusp of exponential growth. He knew it, his creditors knew it. All Harris needed was some time and financial wiggle room.

CHAPTER 28

"**H**ey, Cap'n Moviestar."

Moviestar had changed the spark plugs and distributor cap, added some STP to the gas tank, and then took a ride in the *Miss Ruth*; to make sure she was running right, he'd have claimed. He cruised through Kent Narrows, and buzzed the county slips. Some of the crabbers were down there running their mouths, a couple old salts working on their boats. Burle Shoalwater and Skeeter Philpot sat in Burle's pickup drinking beer.

One of the Tyde boys was helping his daddy, Enoch, with some carpentry. It looked to Moviestar like they were replacing that bad wood around their cabin windows. It was the boy who hollered and waved as Moviestar motored by.

Shoalwater, Philpot, and the Tyde boy were all still just kids— Tooey's age, more or less. In their faces, Moviestar recognized his own youth and the boys that shared it. For a lifetime of days, Moviestar and his contemporaries stood right where those younger men now stood, and had conducted countless conversations, debates, and arguments of their own, telling a library full of tales. Before, and even more so after he'd lost his sons, BS-ing with the boys had been one of Moviestar's greatest joys.

The boys, the ones he grew up with that weren't in the ground, rarely made it down to the slips anymore. Maybe you'd see them at the store, or at a funeral, but that was about it. The thought saddened Moviestar, but the circumstances felt natural, the way things were supposed to go. *His* boys were gone forever and their absence was never going to fit right.

Moviestar scanned the horizon. Starboard, there was a to-do at the yacht club and on the eastern side, by the packing houses and the black American Legion post, Well's Cove was hopping with people too. Out on Prospect Bay there were more pleasure boats than Moviestar ever remembered seeing. It was time to take the *Miss Ruth* in before one of these yahoos in his cigarette boat or cabin cruiser ran clean overtop her without spilling his highball. The patriarchal waterman gave his grandson's workboat a little gas, enough to get her on plane. Moviestar was getting hungry and going home.

Ruth had still been napping when Moviestar left. He was looking forward to eating a late lunch with her. He had four nice soft crabs that he'd fry in the cast iron spider. They'd be juicy where they should and crispy everywhere else. Tomatoes in their garden were ripening, and there were turnips and mustard greens left over from last night's meal. Supper had been different the night before without Tooey, but nice. Just the two of them.

For decades, the rhythm of Moviestar Walter's life had been determined by his devotion to the tides and to his family. He believed he'd done his best raising two of the orneriest urchins anybody ever saw, and he'd tried his damnedest to be a decent stand-in daddy for Tooey. Moviestar had learned many lessons along his voyage, and worked hardest to not always choose the default easiest way out when it came to dealing with the hearts of loved ones.

The calm waters at the mouth of the creek reminded Moviestar of his surface, what people saw when they looked at him, what they based their shallow opinions on, instead of life's true depths, which were, plain and simple, his to harvest as it suited him. The wake from a passing ski boat reminded him how ridiculous it was that at his age and profession he still didn't know how to swim.

Once onshore, Moviestar started his pickup, and headed home. He was happy to have talked to his grandson on the phone earlier. He thought Tooey sounded good, upbeat for a change. The boy had suffered enough knocks in his life, there was no wonder he carried burdens. In recent months—Moviestar scolded himself for not being certain how long—Tooey's flat spirits were of accumulating concern.

Ruth was nervous for Tooey all the time, and ever since he was born. Moviestar would tell her, "Leave it go, Tooey'll do what's right for hisself. He's going to be just fine, valentine." But with the evident weight of Tooey's heavy, dog-tired heart, it was difficult, even for Moviestar, not to fret for him some.

Maybe this opportunity with Bradnox wasn't such a bad thing. He knew Tooey was stuck in neutral, but hadn't understood the boy was questioning his life's work. It saddened Moviestar to think that by assuming a waterman's existence was what his grandson desired he'd had a hand in Tooey's unhappiness.

For a moment, and only a moment, Moviestar regretted not being able to offer Tooey anything but the skills of a waterman in the occupation's twilight. The thought passed with the knowledge that life was what it was. A person deals with whatever comes along in whichever way he knows how. For Moviestar that meant knowing where the most bountiful oyster rocks were and where the fat crabs swam. It meant loving his wife and boys, and doing what was possible to protect and guide his grandchild.

Tooey had felt uneasy associating himself with the big-shot Bradnox. The way Moviestar saw it those were good instincts on Tooey's part. But Tooey craved the world. That's what twenty-year-olds do.

Moviestar Walter never feared much of anything, and he'd never say it out loud, but any thought of losing Tooey cloaked the old man's soul with despair. Far as Moviestar knew he never once let on.

λ

The weeping willow in the front yard was healthy again. Moviestar had removed a diseased limb a few months back. All of Moviestar's boys, his sons and Tooey, had swung from the tree's viney branches like monkeys, like Tarzan, like Batman. The twisted skyscraping oaks in the back yard, fit for climbing since before even Moviestar himself was hatched, survivors of lightning strikes and gall blight, were sometimes all the proof of God's majesty Moviestar ever needed.

The Walter family bungalow, built on the subdivided front tenth of a larger plot, had jalousie windows and shingle siding that wouldn't hold paint without chalking. No one could brush against it without collecting a coating of dust. The shingles on the low-pitched roof were weathered; the framing shifted on its foundation a slice.

To Moviestar, the exterior of their home looked like his old age felt: rundown. Inside, where everything was warm, soft, and well cared for, that was all Ruth.

Moviestar took off his rubber boots and stood in his white-socked feet on the terra cotta tiles of their porch. Hoping his wife was awake so he could share his thoughts, he made a bit more noise than necessary getting in the door with his crabs and tomatoes.

He crossed the front room with a younger man's spring in his step, not seeing or hearing Ruth anywhere until he walked into the kitchen. When Moviestar laid eyes on his steadfast and beloved wife, he stopped dead in his tracks without a moment to speak or even think, and then dropped like an anchor to the floor.

Chapter 29

"**Stop. Enough,**" **Dee** said, each syllable broken glass.

"I'm gonna kick him one more time," said Clacker. He aimed a Red Wing boot at Salt Wade's temple.

"Don't," Dee squeaked. "Help Tooey."

Clacker lifted Tooey to his feet. Tooey was conscious, but not by much. From a breach near his right eye, blood ran down the side of his face.

Clacker took a bandana handkerchief from his hip pocket and wrapped it around Tooey's head. He picked the Oriole's ball cap from the dirt, dusted it, adjusted the plastic strap to help put pressure against the cut, and affixed it to Tooey's dinged crown. He wrapped his arm around Tooey's waist. Dee draped one of Tooey's arms over Clacker's muscular shoulders.

"What about Helmet Head?" Clacker asked Dee.

Dee tumbled it around in her brain, but not for long. "Come on," she said. "Let's get out of here."

On the street, Dee propped Tooey in the doorway of an out-of-business clothing store while Clacker went to get "Blue Lightning." Dee hated how guys named everything. One more way of marking what they considered their territory.

The El Camino's half-car, half-truck design offered just enough cab space for two seats, a gear shift, an overflowing ashtray, and Clacker's bulky CB radio. Dee sat on Tooey's lap. She found a wad of paper napkins in the glove compartment, took off his ball cap, and held the napkins against Tooey's head, wiping away any blood that leaked from Clacker's grungy makeshift bandage.

"Don't let him pass out," Clacker said. "He's probably got a concussion."

"What the hell, Clacker?" Dee's pain was ebbing. "What the hell are you doing here? Where the hell'd you come from?"

Clacker ogled her while he drove. "A thank you'd be nice," he said. "Looked like you two dummies was getting ready to get messed up real good." He nodded at Tooey. "I said, don't let him pass out like that."

She whacked Tooey's cheek harder than necessary.

"Thank you, thank you, thank you,' Dee said. "Now tell me what the hell."

"Your daddy sent him here to get you, and sent me to make sure something like what almost just happened don't, and now we're going back to the Shore." He smiled his broken smile at her. "You got what your daddy's waiting on?"

"No," Dee said, now knowing for certain what everything would come down to between her and her father. "We have to go to my apartment to get it."

⚓

Dee hadn't given Clacker Herbertson a thought in years.

In school Clacker attracted a loyal group of knucklehead toadies who cheered with bootlicking self-preservation every time he bullied somebody other than themselves. Dee understood their type of runty cowardice and despised it. She never knew Clacker not to have backbone. That won him situational points.

Clacker's chest and arms still looked granite solid, his belly much less so. He was as ugly as ever with his humongous, thick-browed head sunburned even in the dark, and that AWOL front tooth. He was already going bald. His breath was dragonesque.

He had on what Dee was sure he considered his 'dress clothes' – a dry-heave disco shirt with long sleeves rolled past his elbow, a not-white-anymore T-shirt underneath. Clacker's pants were the lumpy-pocketed bottom half of a cheap leisure suit. The raised crease on his right knee ran right through a faint grass stain. He wore work boots.

He looked like the dumb, conformist, chauvinist jerk Dee remembered him to be.

She wished she had another Quaalude or ten.

⅄

Clacker knew right off Dee Bradnox was still the pissy spoiled brat she'd always been. She was still good looking too, despite all the trashy make-up and being on the skinny side. Girl could use a sandwich. Her jeans were tighter than two coats of paint, and that thin-strapped top was as sexy as all get-out. A silver chain hung around her neck with a pendant Clacker thought was the Roman numeral two. She wore a bracelet so laden with charms it jingled every time she moved her arm. Clacker thought she looked like a gypsy.

Dee's eyes were the golden brown of un-iced birthday cake. Her hair was a matted mess, and that was one hideous hat, but her lips, promiscuous and capable of spitting poison, were shaped like Clacker's favorite hunting bow. Clacker envisioned Dee asking him for a kiss. Despite his concerns about where those lips of hers may have been, if she did that, asked him for a kiss, he'd pull Blue Lightning over like the motor dropped out.

"Park here," Dee said, sounding as though she thought she was talking to a dog with a driver's license. "Sit and wait," she said. "I'll be right out."

"No." Clacker was not letting her ass out of his sight. "I'm going too."

"What about him?"

"I'll bring Tooey with me. He ain't looking so hot." The bleeding had slowed, but Tooey hadn't spoken since they had gotten in Clacker's car. "I think he needs a doctor."

"He can wait until we get home." Dee said, stepping from the El Camino. As if to counter her assertion, Tooey tilted to the right and vomited all over the sidewalk. Dee jumped out of the line of fire.

"I ain't so sure of that," Clacker said.

Clacker helped Tooey maneuver the stairwell, as Dee led the way. In the hallway on the third floor, Dee unlocked a wall cubby. She reached in and pulled out what looked to Clacker like a cigar box, but metal, with a handle, and the size of a camp stove.

"While we're here I want a couple things from my apartment," Dee told Clacker. "Bring him," she said, poking Tooey in the chest, almost tipping him. Tooey took a step back and puked again.

"Oh, man," Tooey said. "I think I'm going to…"

"Black out," said Clacker, catching Tooey, nothing but body parts in a damp paper bag, on his way down.

Dee's apartment was shed-sized, stifling hot, and overturned to boot. Behind some beads, Clacker righted her capsized cot with one hand and dumped Tooey on top, covering him with a blanket Clacker assumed had been knitted by a crippled blind kid.

Clacker lit a cigarette. He plopped into a violence-perforated beanbag chair and Styrofoam pellets volcanoed into the air from a number of slits. A touchtone telephone in the image of a celebrity rodent lay on the linoleum floor, his cord cut and his ears busted off. Dee placed the weird-looking case on a mutilated loveseat out of Clacker's easy reach while she threw clothing and personal effects into several plastic shopping bags. "Don't get comfortable," she had the nerve to say.

"He needs a doctor," Clacker said.

"We don't have time," said Dee.

"We'd have plenty of time if you'd let me kick that guy some more," Clacker said. "Who the hell was that?"

"A friend."

"Glad he ain't my friend." Clacker rubbed his face to camouflage the uncontrollable calisthenics his tics were busy inventing and said, "He a tough dude?"

"Yeah. That's not the first time somebody kicked his ass some. He'll be meaner when he gets up."

"Screw that guy." Clacker said. "Tooey's probably got a concussion. A bad concussion ain't nothing to shake off. I've had a few playing football and—"

"Well, that's obvious."

Clacker ignored the shot. "—Tooey could blink out, not wake up. Your friend Helmet Head—"

"Salt."

"Salt?"

"It's his name, what do you want me to do about it, *Clacker?*"

"Your friend, *Salt*, ain't going nowhere for a while, and it looks like he's already stopped by here, anyway. You know an emergency room close, any doctors we could take Tooey to?"

From his cot, Tooey began to sing. Loud. After a minute, Clacker said, "Oh my god, you have got to get him some help or I'm gonna go in there and put a pillow over his face. What the hell is that?"

"I think it's *"Doctor My Eyes"* by Jackson Browne," Dee said.

"Doctor, my fucking ears," said Clacker.

Chapter 30

All Tooey wanted was to awaken. Eyes as heavy as a Black Sabbath song, his backstage curtain refused to rise. The cavernous concert-hall in his head, built with rebar, Jell-O, and ammonia fumes, was dry-well empty except for Tooey, Tooey's grandmother, and Kiss guitarist Ace Frehley flying around on a kiddie ride biplane. Ma stood in a darkened alcove off to one side. She wouldn't look Tooey's way.

In a flash, a turn of the channel, Tooey was sitting on the bow of the *Miss Ruth*, the most calming spot on earth. Trouble was, the boat was stranded at the top of a colossal pine tree, broken mid-keel and sliding off. The voices echoing through the surrounding evergreen forest spoke in tongues.

He slept until he wondered if he was awake, back to a reality he might recognize. He knew for sure he was laid out on the thinnest mattress in any possible universe. The pillowcase was clammy with sweat against his neck. He moved his eyes but didn't lift his head. There wasn't much to see anyway, a corner and a curtain of hippie beads.

Tooey closed down.

He heard a faint noise. Peeking, he saw a girl standing in profile, at the foot of the bed, a beautiful girl. Dee, Dee Bradnox. The details were fuzz-covered but Tooey could, to a degree, recall the events that had brought him and Dee Bradnox into a room together.

Dee stood a few feet away. Slivers of light radiated in from past the beaded curtain, and fell across her features like a gift.

He noticed her blouse was bloodied. Tooey felt close to Dee in that moment but couldn't quite put together why. A choppy Chesapeake Bay crossed his mind, something about undertow. Dee took her top off. Tooey's addled thoughts washed out to sea. Her breasts were full and firm, the nipples silhouetted in the room's glow. Her hair was down and she stretched her body straight as she took in a deep, fatigued breath. She knelt. Tooey watched from behind one squinted eye.

Dee stood and slipped on a navy T-shirt. She disappeared through the beads. As existence again faded, Tooey was able to confirm one body part that still worked even if his brain circuits were no longer holding a charge.

⚔

Dee went downstairs to Mr. Toy's corner liquor store and called The Block Doc. Abortions, overdoses, and the clap were Dr. Henry Merriman's specialties, but concussions could not be far out of his area of expertise. According to Salt, Dr. Henry had been the doctor for Julius Cornwall's vice empire since the 1950s, performing procedures The Lord Cornwall preferred to keep out of the hands and record-keeping of more legitimate medical practitioners. Head wounds, Dee presumed, had to be on Dr. Henry's list of services rendered.

She let the phone ring a bunch of times, disconnected, tried again, and got him on the third attempt. After she made the call, Dee, clenching the case as tight as Salt Wade ever did, thought about checking Clacker's stupid-looking truck-car to see if he'd left the keys behind. She instead decided to stick with the boys.

CHAPTER 31

Henry Merriman was coming down. Sensory awareness returned through his body's relationship with a straight back chair. An astronaut on reentry, his mortal capsule, outside blazing, arctic winter on the inside, broke atmospheres in an earthbound free-fall.

A layer of infinite space expanded between the rosewood furniture, his shirt, and his skin. Henry thought he might drift off yet again until he heard those cavities of air hissing, leaking. With their deflation, the Art Nouveau antique in which he sat bonded to his anatomy with such resolve Henry knew he couldn't be extracted with the Jaws of Life.

His eyes opened. He grew mindful of his surroundings. He began to acknowledge physical actualities. The yellowed plaster wall across the room, the color of tobacco stain, grew more focused, the perfume of decay more pronounced.

Henry was conscious of inhaling oxygen. It did not sit well on his palate.

When he was able to lift his arm, Henry sipped watered-down, bottom-shelf brandy from a coffee cup. It burned like gasoline despite the cut.

The Fentanyl, however, was exceptional. A hundred times stronger than morphine, and mixed with a touch of benzodiazepine to take the edge off, Henry's synthetic narcotic concoction possessed such superlative hypnotic qualities that it rendered even this bargain basement swill potable. Despite constant flulike symptoms, and the occasional hallucination seeping into his sober cognizance, Henry's self-prescribed and homemade evening tranquilizer was his life's singular pleasure.

⅄

Federal Hill had always been considered several strata down from the gilded, aloof environs across town where Henry's family resided. Now this section of Baltimore had deteriorated to the point Mayor Schaefer was selling uninhabited houses for a dollar.

Overlooking the Patapsco River's northwest branch, Federal Hill was once a thriving workingman's community, the historic heart of Baltimore's industry and defense. Nearby Fort McHenry had guarded the city's most vital point of entry for almost as long as there'd been a United States of America.

From the days of the Clipper ships through the World War II steel and iron boom, the denizens of Federal Hill were capitalists, craftsmen, and seaworthy salt of the earth.

The defined opposite of Henry Merriman.

By the 1960s, Federal Hill's well-paid industrial jobs were history. So was the life Henry was supposed to have lived. Both had been gouged far beyond what felt fair.

A few residences on Henry's street, once one of the community's most distinguished thoroughfares, had been purchased and renovated by homesteaders taking advantage of the city's investment program. The Merriman row house, though never abandoned like some of the proximate structures, had felt hollowed out for years. The damage and rot were obvious and pervasive.

The property had been in Henry's family for more than a century and was held for him in trust. Three and a half stories, the attic room featured a huge window with an expansive water view. Sometimes, but not tonight, Henry would inject drugs while gazing out that window, and imagine himself a successful 18th century adventurer.

Tonight, Henry was once again where he didn't like to go but never left.

Henry was the unclaimed black sheep of his wealthy and well-connected family. His paternal grandfather was one of Johns Hopkins Medical School's first professors; his father, William, a renowned research surgeon at the same prestigious institution. William would have governed his household in the Victorian tradition if not for Henry's mother, older than her spouse and the daughter of a distinguished general. Marjorie Booth Merriman, too progressive for her husband's pompous and outdated sensibilities, insisted on working outside the home, and served as a director of the Hopkins nursing school for thirty years. Henry's older brother was a Hopkins honors graduate, a leading cardiologist, and a decorated war veteran. Their sisters, twins married to prominent physicians, were dedicated to retaining the family's stature at the top of Baltimore's privileged class.

For many years, Henry did his best not to disappoint his loved ones.

School had been difficult. Henry could not live up to his family's standards.

Henry reported for his physical toward the end of World War II and went 4-F. He always speculated his mother had exerted influence to get the Army to absolve him of service, but she would never admit to pulling such strings.

In 1954, working in the Hopkins emergency room and still living in his parents' home, thirty five year old Henry Merriman was caught sending love letters to a twelve year old neighbor boy. The scandal was meteoric, burning bright and fleet. Henry's parents used their ample prestige and resources to stifle the attention of the police, press, and courts, and Henry was confined to an Eastern Shore mental hospital for two years.

Upon Henry's return to Baltimore, his parents explained that he would be allowed to reside in their unoccupied Federal Hill row house but was unwelcome in Mt. Vernon. He could have no contact with any family members. In a depressive and frantic attempt to substantiate his sexual harmlessness, Dr. Henry Booth Merriman performed a self-castration surgery.

He cut off his own testicles to prove a point.

Henry spent another thirty months institutionalized.

Within months of his second release, Henry met Julius Cornwall through a street dealer, and gained the crime lord's confidence by becoming The Block's go-to "sawbones." In his career, Henry had removed more bullets than some dentists pulled teeth, and he'd stitched together more body parts than Dr. Frankenstein.

Henry's parents were in their eighties now, still very much alive and active amongst Maryland's senior Democratic leaders, but Henry had neither seen nor spoken to them in two decades. Their attorney forwarded his monthly stipend without interruption.

The telephone rang and Henry's once elegant row home, otherwise silent, and haunted by the almost-dead, shuddered at the intrusion.

Henry resisted answering, but his pharmaceutical orbit was complete, he'd survived splashdown and been hauled in by the Navy. He was a doctor after all, and from the caller's persistence, someone somewhere required his skills. If that caller had cash money handy, the good Dr. Merriman would be at their service.

CHAPTER 32

Henry called Frank, a cab driver who gave the doctor rides no charge. They had an arrangement.

Frank waited outside while Henry went upstairs. Inside the wrecked apartment, a burly young man pointed to a curtain of hanging beads and said, "They're back there."

Henry recognized Salt Wade's one-of-a-kind carrying case tucked behind the edge of the loveseat as soon as he walked through the door. He'd recently treated one of Salt's streetwalkers for an infection. The case and its riches were all Salt could talk about.

He parted the makeshift room divider. The girl everybody called Heaven wiped blood from a second young man's brow.

"Thanks for coming, Dr. Henry," Heaven said.

"What happened?"

"He fell," she said. She appeared distraught.

"Much blood?"

"A lot less than it looked like there was going to be at first."

"Has he been unconscious since... he fell?"

"No. He's been in and out. Mostly in, a little bit."

"Acting goofier than usual," said the big kid from the other side of the beads.

Henry roused the patient, and asked his name. The boy's answer was swift, robotic. "Wesley Walter the second," he said.

"The second? Not junior?"

"Not junior. Tooey. WW Tooey." The patient appeared rational to a degree.

Opening his satchel, Henry said, "I'm a doctor, Wesley. I'm going to take your blood pressure."

"Don't take it all."

"Would you excuse us please?" Henry said to Heaven. She stepped away. Henry was having a hard time not thinking about the carrying case he'd seen. "Blood pressure's low," he said, "but within normal range. How do you feel?"

"Not quite right. You?"

"I'm well, thank you. Do you have a headache or nausea?"

"Yes, sir. My head hurts most. Hard to think straight. I threw up."

"You need stitches and have a moderate to severe concussion. I recommend you go to the hospital." The patient slipped out of consciousness and Henry felt this was as good a time as any to stitch the stupid bastard.

⅄

One of these days, Tooey thought, when I come to, when I'm able to focus a minute, I'm going to figure out where I've seen this man before.

The doctor looked like hell—papery skin, a boozer's tremble, and long ratty gray hair tied in a rattier ponytail. Maybe it was the dim light of wherever it was they were, but there was a familiarity about this man that called himself doctor.

Dr. Phibes maybe, Tooey snickered, then stopped and said, "Wait, what?"

"Your friends say you fell," said the doctor.

"I fell." Tooey thought maybe he did take a splat somewhere along the line. "Ass over tin cups," Tooey said. There was a plastic radio playing inside Tooey's head. Every so often somebody would turn the dial, but the reception seemed to be clearing. "I feel sick to my stomach," he told the doctor.

"That can happen," the doctor said and foot-pushed an empty cardboard box Tooey's way. "If it continues, you have to go a hospital. How do you feel otherwise?"

"Splitting headache." Tooey pawed his gauzed temple.

The doctor read his expression and said, "That's where you fell. You suffered a minor contusion that required sutures."

"Oh yeah? I don't remember that," Tooey said.

"What do you remember?" the doctor asked.

"I remember before you were here."

"How about the president? Do you know who the president is?"

"Ford."

"What holiday is tomorrow?

Tooey concentrated through static. "Fourth of July. You said friends?"

"Excuse me?"

"My friends said I fell? Who friends? Dee and..."

"Hey, Tooey, it's me." That voice. The same rumble Tooey thought he'd heard in the dreaming place. It was a challenge to sort out while spinning up and down the radio dial inside his cranium. Who said what again?

"Your vision is normal? You're not seeing double?"

Tooey smacked his lips, "My mouth tastes nasty."

"Take these two Tylenol. Two more every two hours. I want you to go to the emergency room, especially if your symptoms don't diminish, if you vomit again, or grow feverish. You can rest, but someone should wake you regularly for the next twenty-four hours. Prolonged sleep is not good. Your cut should heal. That will be forty dollars."

Tooey fished money from his hip pocket.

"Are there any other questions?"

"Uhm, yes sir," Tooey said, "Could you maybe tell me who's out there other than Dee? I have to try and focus here. That guy sounds like he could hurt somebody."

The doctor called to Dee. She came back and stood beside Tooey, took his hand in hers, and listened while the doctor repeated instructions.

The doctor parted the beaded curtain and vanished.

Dee stood next to Tooey and held his hand.

CHAPTER 33

Dee grabbed her bags, told Clacker, "Get him and let's get going. Doc says no problem. Tooey's not going to die on us before we get him home."

"We'll keep him up," Clacker said. "It's better if he don't sleep. Got your crap?"

"Give me your shirt."

"Why?"

"Tooey's is all bloody. You've got your T-shirt. None of mine will fit him."

"You trying to get me naked, Delores?" said Clacker, gap-toothed and grinning.

Dee rolled her eyes and took Clacker's roomy polyester eyesore from him. She stuck her head through the beads. "Hey, Tooey, it's time to leave, go home." She thought he replied, but he made no attempt to move. She walked over and kicked the cot's frame. "Tooey! Come on, let's go!"

Tooey sat up like somebody touched a Zippo to the soles of his feet. He looked around with an odd expression, groaned, and swung his legs off the mattress. Dee handed him Clacker's shirt. She walked back into her living area and to the loveseat.

Her heart stopped. She gasped.

"What's wrong?" Clacker asked.

"Tell me you have it."

"What?" Clacker asked.

"The case, dipstick." Dee went to a quick low simmer. "The fancy case, the metal one, looks a cross between a cigar box and a lunch pail?"

"That creepy Marcus Welby must have grabbed it," Clacker groaned.

"How?" Dee stomped. "How could Dr. Henry have taken the case?"

"I had to pee."

"What?"

"Y'all were with Tooey. I ducked into the bathroom for like a second."

"A second?"

"I," Clacker glared at her, daring her to push him, "had to pee. You never said watch that case or nothing. I wasn't on guard duty."

"A second? That little thing of yours empties out quick, huh?"

Tooey walked through the beads, Clacker's shirt covering him like a tarp. "We going home?" he asked.

人

In the moments Tooey's head was clearest, his spine ached like he'd been racked. It didn't help that three people were scrunched into two bucket seats. Every time he got comfortable, Dee, sitting on his lap, would adjust and undo all his effort.

The night was muggy. Clacker and Dee were at each other the whole time; wouldn't shut up. They needed the case, okay, Tooey understood that, but could they maybe just relax, listen to the radio?

"I can't believe," Dee kept on, "you couldn't wait until he was gone before you went wee-wee. Your bladder must be weaker than your brain."

"Yeah, well, *I* can't believe your doctor's a zombie, and that you left all that money out like it was milk and cookies."

"Money?"

"The money in the case."

"Who said anything about money?" Dee motioned left.

Clacker ran the light and made the turn. "I'm not stupid, Dee-lores. I know you think you're a step ahead of everybody all the time, but you ain't. You got money in that case. You owe your daddy and you're paying him back so you can come home. So now, because Tooey got slammed into a wall—"

"A fence."

"—by the man you stole the money from, you had to call in that creep who basically told us not to let Tooey die, then stole the money. If Tooey wasn't already starting to act like his weird ass self, I'd be saying screw you and driving him to the emergency room instead. You doing all right there, Too?"

For background music, Tooey was transmitting a Blue Oyster Cult album on his brain's AM/FM. The car hit a bump and he lost the signal. Tooey pulled himself together, tried to straighten in his seat, and said, "No prob-lem-o."

Clacker drove through a busy neighborhood where there were lots of people, most heading in one direction. Cars were parked curbside and in vacant lots. Clacker pulled into a roped off square, and paid the attendant one dollar.

Dee led Tooey and Clacker against the pedestrian stream. Clacker said, "Where the hell these dweebs going?"

"I don't know," said Dee. "Fort McHenry maybe. It's right down there."

Tooey announced, "Ed McMahon is there with a giant birthday cake." He thought he was being informative.

"I'm telling you we should have taken him to the hospital," Clacker said.

"My back hurts," said Tooey.

Chapter 34

Henry Merriman's row house felt like a cave-in. The foursquare architecture and roaring twenties décor added to the heft of times gone by. Ornamental marble attested to the home's long-past grandeur, plywood over the broken window spoke to its current condition. The case, cumbersome with the pressure of possibility, lay on the doctor's lap with paralyzing effect.

The case was decorated with a landscape, a cypress swamp forest with baying canines under a cloudy sky and cratered moon. On the bottom, under an inconspicuous sliding plate, was a four-dial combination lock.

Henry took a sip of brandy, and wiped his watery eyes with the back of his wrist. He wondered what he should do. He knew how to contact the man the case ostensibly belonged to, but Henry didn't like Salt, never had. Returning the case would buy favor with the ambitious and connected dealer, but if what Salt had been boasting around town was true, this case might contain fortune enough to provide Henry comfort in whatever time he had left to endure his miserable life.

Henry sat at the foot of his bed. He'd always been frail, but in the mirror across the room he was skeletal. His skin was pockmarked and pallid, his head an inverted triangle. His eyes were deep-set, his lips thin, his dingy teeth crooked from grinding day and night. His linen suit was frayed and out of fashion.

Henry watched himself scratch his own neck with a compulsion soothed somewhat by lighting one of his long brown cigarettes.

He fantasized where he would travel for his last exquisite binge, where he might end life as an anonymous overdose on a beach or in a woodlands someplace. The doctor was certain that if he were to cease to exist, not just die as some inconvenience, but disappear, his family would suffer immense guilt for how they'd treated him.

That's what he decided he'd do once he was able to open Salt Wade's case.

Henry wished he wasn't who he was, wished his family still loved him. He sat there with the ponderous case, thinking about the Johns Hopkins motto, "Veritas Vos Liberabit." Henry knew now that no truth ever set anyone free. Truth confined.

Tremorous with the pins and needles of addiction, Henry's judgment boomeranged. He decided to return the case to the girl called Heaven. He told himself it was the right thing to do, and though he struggled with obvious impulse issues, a Merriman almost always did what was right upon taking time to think.

Before finishing off the liquor in his coffee cup, Henry held a silent toast to the only person he'd ever loved outside his family. A little boy long since grown to be a man, somewhere out in the world with a life Henry hoped was happy. Normal. A once innocent and beautiful child Henry loved but never laid a finger on.

Henry never in his life touched another person in a sexual manner. He castrated himself to prove he never would.

There was a sharp, insistent knock at Henry Merriman's front door.

CHAPTER 35

The street was less well lit here, less busy. Tooey stood with Dee and Clacker on the sidewalk in front of the doctor's house, a Charles Addams structure from crumbled pavement to warped roof. The brick front was the color of dead, soot-coated roses. Rotted shutters hung on without optimism. The marble steps were green with vegetation and the rusted wrought iron handrail wobbly, the paint on the front door blistered and cracked like a burn victim's skin. "Salt brought me here once," was all Dee said.

"In a hearse?" Clacker asked. Dee pounded on the door.

The door opened and Dr. Henry stepped to one side, throwing his arm out in an exaggerated gesture and moaning in a voice from the grave, "Come in, come in." For Tooey, it was like being greeted by a lethargic late night monster movie host.

Clacker mumbled, "You got to be kidding me." The foyer reeked of neglect.

Dee said, "I can't believe you stole from me, Dr. Henry. Give me the case."

"I know, Heaven. I feel abominable," Henry fidgeted. "I was just about to return the case. I know it's not yours, but it's not mine either. I'd appreciate you not mentioning my lapse in judgment to your boyfriend."

Tooey could tell Dee wasn't listening. "So where is it?" she said.

"Upstairs," said Henry. "Excuse me while I go get it."

"I'll go with you," Dee said.

"You're not going up there alone with this freak," Clacker said. "Come on, Tooey," Clacker shoved Tooey. Tooey appreciated the prodding. He'd blinked out.

The quartet climbed a staircase to the second and third story, each flight more squalid and threadbare than the last, and every stride sapping more of Tooey's waning energy.

Henry said, "The case is in my bedroom."

Dee started to follow. Clacker held his arm out, stopped her. He shook his head. Dee went, "tuh," and rolled her eyes, but didn't step past. Tooey checked his watch. It was a little before midnight and orange. His ring was pinkish. He inspected his pockets for the mood chart but it was gone. A sucker once again.

Henry walked back into the hall, protecting the case like a running back, like he'd changed his mind. He started back down the dark, grimy stairway.

"Hey, Dr. Henry," Dee said, "don't get too attached to that thing. It's mine."

Henry was two steps ahead of Dee, Tooey and Clacker behind her. On the landing between floors, Henry stopped and turned. Dee reached out, grasped the case's handle. "That's interesting," Henry said, releasing the case and allowing Dee to take possession. "I thought it belonged to Salt Wade. Did he give it to you?"

A male figure stepped from the stairwell's pit of shadows. He said, "Answer the man, Heaven. Did Salt Wade give you his case?"

147

CHAPTER 36

After his beating, Salt Wade had dragged himself to a corner phone booth. It took a while. He called a chummy taxi service, and went home where he cleaned and fixed himself the best he could.

Though his bottom lip was split, his face swelling and turning passion fruit purple in places, his nose was intact, his vision keen. The bones under the skin felt unbroken. He could breathe but the deep breaths hurt. A splintered stinging tormented his ribcage and insisted on not letting him forget the jackhammers he'd taken to his torso. There was sporadic ringing in his ears.

Salt needed a doctor.

Howlin' Lobo slithered and crunched his way through Salt's high-end speakers. Expressing the sound of a trampled underdog's pain and defiance, the Lobo's Blues were the bruised, bitter rumblings that bloomed in a soul unafraid of certain gospel truths. The system's crooked. No one can hope to survive untainted. The cross-eyed darkness that burrows deep inside the aggrieved man needs room to breathe fire or it will explode.

There was something in the Blues that made it sound that way. The Blues had to be devil music because it told the truth. Salt found his own insight comforting.

He huffed lines off a glass coffee table, and slipped his diamond-sharp Buck knife into the holster he hung from the belt of his sullied jumpsuit. He hadn't been hunting in years. He turned off his stereo, taking care to return the record to its sleeve, and grabbed a cassette he'd recorded at the Ann Arbor Blues Festival. Downstairs, he hotwired his neighbor's van, a porthole-windowed Chevy adorned with airbrushed amateur paintings of mermaids resembling Robert Mitchum, but with long hair, tits, and fishtails.

The Lobo played live on tape all the way to Federal Hill. Driving through the doctor's neighborhood, Salt saw the streets crawling with Baltimore County family types. He remembered some Bicentennial observance was going down at Fort McHenry. On a normal Saturday night these civic and safety minded folks wouldn't be caught anywhere near this neck of the city.

Salt spotted Heaven from a block away. She was scurrying like a rat against the current. Her puppy-boy tagged along, and there was a second, beefier asshole with them, a tank. Tank must have been the sucker-puncher. Salt owed that fatso big time.

None of the three stooges carried Salt's case.

He knew where they must be going. He hoped he'd hurt Heaven and the kid enough that they required more of Henry Merriman's bad doctoring than Salt himself did. Driving past Dr. Henry's rundown row house, Salt parked the van in a tow-zone, snorted from his vial, and hustled into the night to scope things out.

Under the city's real estate rehab program, a rookie city cop, a uniformed patrolman with a straight-arrow reputation, had moved in next door to the doctor. Everybody knew it, so Dr. Henry rarely saw patients at home anymore.

An empty blue and white police car sat parked at the corner. Salt staked out a darkened doorway across the street. There was no activity visible at either house until Heaven and her flunkies approached.

Salt slipped into the back alley. One light was on inside the lawman's house, a ceiling fixture in the ground floor kitchen where the window was raised, held open with an adjustable screen. Except for fan-blown curtains there was no movement to be seen, nor a peep of sound. And yet Salt believed he sensed a presence inside.

Dr. Henry's unlit backyard was overgrown with weeds. The gate swung open like an invitation to an entombment. Standing on a rusted metal lawn chair, his injuries protesting all the way, Salt climbed onto the roof of the low-pitched, one-story addition. He crept up to reach a second level window that opened with the faintest creak. Salt stretched with pain, and slid over the sill. The doctor's house smelled like a hospital left to fester.

Salt heard voices. The conversation grew louder and clearer as he eased across the bedroom floor. Heaven and Dr. Henry passed by, and Salt glued himself to the door. Dr. Henry was speaking, trying to say he was sorry for taking the case, but Heaven was tearing into him. What a conniving skank she was, Salt thought, complaining about somebody ripping off something she'd swiped too.

Heaven berated Dr. Henry all the way up the stairs. The two knuckleheads stomped by, one saying how much he didn't like the feeling of this, and the other humming along like he was in some kind of happy-dappy Uncle Remus movie.

They all sounded stupid to Salt.

Salt had never killed anybody. He'd come close a couple times, and he'd witnessed more than one soul wave bye-bye to their worldly carcass, but it was clear that tonight this whole batch of idiots would have to die by his hand.

Salt vacuumed a pile of coke from tip of his knife, and stepped into the hallway.

CHAPTER 37

Tooey had been thinking he was going to get to go home. Time had folded and unfolded, flipped and back-flipped, plus he was as tired as he'd ever been, but as soon as the man from the abyss spoke, Tooey's vision straightened and his focus cleared.

Home left the picture.

Dee took several steps backward. She was so close Tooey smelled her hair. It smelled terrific.

The man with the big knife and bigger hair rephrased his question. "Well, did I?" He pretzeled Dr. Henry into a half-nelson and gripped the left side of the doctor's face with the iron clasp of his palm. The doctor's knees buckled. The man glared over Henry's shoulder, his mug busted and scowling. "Did I, Salt Wade, give you my case?"

Salt's voice never raised a fraction of a decibel, but when he next spoke there was a roar of tone. "Answer me, Heaven. Did I? Did I give it to you? Does that case you're holding on to like it was a baby belong to you?"

"Give it back to him," a slumping Dr. Henry sniveled, glancing back and forth between Dee and the gleaming knife hovering at his cheek.

"That's not a bad idea, Heaven," Salt said. "Give it back. It'll be your chance to do the decent thing for once. You know, return the property to its rightful owner."

"Hey, Helmet Head," Clacker hollered, moving between Salt and Dee, "your best bet is letting that dried up piece of dung go, stepping aside, and letting us be on our way."

"How you figure that?" Salt wanted to know. Tooey caught the Dixie twang.

"Because fucking with me *cannot* end good for you." Clacker pulled a ladylike derringer from his front pants pocket, and pointed it at Salt's puffy countenance. Tooey stopped humming and watched Dee's expression gush astonishment.

"You got a lot of brass," was all that Salt said in response. He forced Dr. Henry's posture straighter, the doctor's eyes opening wide. Henry turned and tried to struggle away, putting the two men at a ninety-degree angle. Salt rose up on his toes, and rotating his wrist, he plunged his blade straight down into the life-or-death tangle of infrastructure between Henry's collarbone and shoulder muscle.

Henry grunted and went limp as Salt wrenched the knife from his flesh. Blood gurgled out like a low-grade science class volcano. Salt dropped the doctor's body into the stairwell's inky murk. Tooey saw the shadows thicken and pulse with the sacrifice.

Clacker pulled the trigger on his pistol.

Nothing happened.

He pulled again without results.

Salt stumbled on the stairway in a clumsy thrust forward. Tooey, Dee, and Clacker turned, and raced back to the third floor, Dee leading the retreat.

Clacker stopped at the top of the stairs, swept a lamp and a stack of books from the lid of an ornate butler's console, and tipped the heavy cabinet down the steps. Salt squawked but there was no crash. The hindrance would be temporary.

Frantic moments passed in slow motion.

A memory popped into Tooey's head. When his father was alive, one of their favorite things to do together was explore the scads of abandoned Eastern Shore farm and manor houses. Wesley Walter the first called this trespassing "hunting for treasure." Whether they ever found any or not depended on how a person defined treasure.

Many of those forsaken but once dignified structures featured a back staircase for access to servants' quarters. A boxy alcove stood at the end of the doctor's hallway. Tooey pointed. Dee's eyes lit with recognition and she flew.

Tooey and Clacker almost crashed into her when she threw on the brakes.

The stairwell to the levels below had been sealed off long ago.

Salt was on the third floor now too, barreling, foaming at the mouth.

There were steps going up. Dee seized them in leaps. The boys followed.

At the front of the long, narrow attic corridor was a wall partition, a door, a room. Salt bounded up the steps behind them. Dee darted to the room and she was in. Clacker pushed Tooey through. He himself cleared the threshold by a hair before Dee slammed the door shut and flung the deadbolt into place.

The room was hot and empty except for one grimy parlor chair near a dormered bay window with a stained glass setting sun. Moldy wallpaper hung from the ceiling in long strips that brushed Tooey's ears and collar. A parched, stagnant odor got in his nose.

Soon it was all he could smell and taste.

Chapter 38

Tooey's concussed brain started spinning again. He'd seen Salt gaining on them before they'd entered the room, a human crustacean with a lethal first-strike defense. The knife in Salt's hand looked like part of a claw, his skin, armored shell and whiteleather.

Drained, Tooey slid down to the crummy floorboards.

There was a pounding from the other side of the door. The door took it like a champ. Salt growled, "I know you hear me, you sonsabitches. Unlock this door right now and I won't walk away and torch what's behind me."

Dee stood over Tooey's prostrate body and replied through the paneled wood. "I've got the case. You're not setting anything on fire. As long as I've got this, I'm safe."

"Oh, but soon as you don't, and that's coming pronto, girl, well, like my mama would say, may God release you from the burdens of this sinful world and unto heaven above—" he took a long pause, "—or not. Either way you're dead meat, Heaven. Them inbred looking friends of yours too."

"Up yours," Clacker told Salt.

"What he said," Tooey whispered to a sliver of light under the door.

Clacker pulled the string to a bare overhead bulb. He mumbled with Dee in the 40-watt gloom. Tooey tracked the conversation with intermittent resolve.

Dee said, "All along you had a gun? In your pocket?"

"I test-fired that hunk of junk, too," Clacker said. "Who would give a guy a gun that don't fire right every shot? Who would do that?"

"Why would you not tell me you had a gun?" Dee asked without waiting for an answer. "Jesus, Clacker, then you pull the thing and it won't even fire? What the hell?"

"What are we going to do?" Clacker asked.

"You and Tooey have to open that door and jump him."

"You're kidding, right?" Clacker pointed. "Tooey ain't worth squirt."

"Give Tooey the gun," Dee said. "You're bigger than Salt. You can take him."

"So you want me to blitz this Salt, this killer with his enormous bloody knife," Clacker said, "with no weapon of my own, but Tooey covers me with a gun that don't work. Unless it does, which means Tooey'll probably shoot me in the back. Meanwhile, you scramble away with a case full of money?"

"You again with the money! Maybe it's my jewelry collection, dumbass, or maybe I have blackmail pictures of Salt humping a giraffe at the city zoo. Whatever it is," Dee said, "it's none of your business, so you should just put a cork in it."

Clacker said, "You don't know, do you?"

"Don't know what?"

"You stole that case and don't even know what's in it. Risked all our lives for you don't know what." Clacker pointed again, "Got that old man out there killed. You see that? How d'you like knowing he's been trenched open and it's all your fault?"

There was dead air for what seemed a month. Tooey's ring and watch were dark as unplugged TV screens. His back ached in waves.

Clacker said, "We should break out this window, yell to somebody, get the cops."

"No, no cops," Dee said. "The cops come and everything goes crazy."

"*Goes* crazy?"

Dee said, "Salt doesn't want the cops—"

"Well," Clacker interrupted, "he killed a dude so I can understand that."

"—and I don't either," Dee said. "Cops get involved, I lose the case. I won't be able to go home. I'll be out of options."

"Your father won't care," said Clacker. "He's your father. Let's do it. Let's throw this chair out that gigantic window and get us some attention."

"My father wants what is in this case, Clacker. Without it we let Daddy down." Her voice vibrated soft. "You don't want to let him down do you?"

Tooey closed his eyes and hummed the national anthem to himself.

"And you're right," Dee admitted. "I don't exactly know what's in here, I can't get it open and I'm afraid to bang it up trying, but what's inside is the most valuable thing Salt's ever seen. We can't go home without it. I can't."

Chapter 39

Tooey heard Salt say with a humorless snicker, "I got all night and the rest of my life. All you three have is the rest of your lives.

"You know what's funny, Heaven?" Salt said. "That ain't even the real case 'cause I got the real one. The reason I'm going to chop you and your friends into itty-bitties is 'cause you had the au-damned-dacity to steal from me. From me."

"Bullshit," Dee said.

"Open it. See for yourself."

"Jerk."

"Either one of you dimwits even know about Howlin' Lobo?" Salt asked without preamble. "*Smokestack Shine? Killing Yard?* The Lobo was the greatest Bluesman ever lived. Never got the credit he deserved. Died a few months back. You know what killed him?"

"No," said Tooey, and Dee kicked Tooey's leg.

"Disco," Salt said. "Know what's going to kill you?"

Dee kicked Tooey before he could answer.

Salt said, "Me. Know how? I'm going to take you out to the country and I'm going to tie you to trees. I'm going to pour gasoline down your gullets, and throw matches in. While your insides burn I'm going to shoot parts off you." Tooey listened to Salt consider alternate savageries.

"Or I might gut you right in that room," Salt said, "and let them find you nekkid with the kid-raper downstairs."

Tooey hummed. Despite the threats Salt spewed, there was pleasantness in his soothing and heartfelt southern voice.

"Poor old Lobo," Salt said after a time, leaving the name hang. "Wasn't no great guitar player, but what he had was his voice and his harps. Nobody came close to what was going on when Howlin' Lobo sang or blew harmonica."

Salt said, "The harmonica," and Tooey couldn't help but sway like Stevie Wonder, "was carried by Pan if you learnt anything in school. Could bewitch anybody what heard it. Only the human voice carries more hoodoo."

Tooey waited for more. He had no idea what Dee and Clacker were thinking during this lesson on the Blues, but Tooey was into it.

Salt continued, "Chinks have been blowing into bamboo for thousands of years, but the Krauts invented the mouth organ," Salt told his captive audience. "The harp's a ventriloquist. Mimics turkeys, foxes, hounds. Wailing trains. Loneliness. Perfect instrument for Bluesmen. Cowboys. Soldiers, too."

After a bit, Salt veered, "The Lobo was born in Mississippi. One quarter full-blood Choctaw. Like me. Choctaws are hard people. Fighters.

"White settlers gave harmonicas to the Indian tribes as peace offerings. Peace offerings – ha! You know Billy the Kid played harp? Abe Lincoln, too."

"When the Blues come along, a harp was so cheap even a black sharecropper could get his hands on one. The Blues don't got no rules. Noise is what the Blues is, playing between the notes of diddley bow guitars with a knife blade or a broken bottle.

"You know when you're afraid and you get that pain in your stomach?" Salt asked. "That gut-punch-kick-in-the-balls ache that makes you want to ralph? You probably got it right now. Well, imagine that feeling all the time. The Blues is all the time."

Tooey was conflicted. He wanted out of this attic, this predicament, but if truth be told, even if he did keep nodding off, Tooey was enjoying Salt's music history class.

Salt was on the floor. His voice came in under the door. "You listening?"

Tooey whispered, "Uh-huh". And as with a goodnight story, he listened until he couldn't keep his eyes open. He decided to try and take a snooze. In the meanwhile, maybe somebody else could figure out what to do next.

Chapter 40

Dee sat in the far corner, on the floor with her arms wrapped around her knees and Salt's case against her chest. The longer Salt rambled on about those dead field hollerers of his, the more she could tell he was coked to the gills.

She hoped he'd snort enough to kill himself.

Clacker sat in the chair looking out the Clacker-sized window.

Tooey was a rug.

Salt talked drums. Dee had fucked a few drummers. She never cared about the music much. She just loved to rock and roll.

"Hillbillies don't like the sounda' drums," Salt said. "Real country music ain't nothing but guitar, fiddle, banjo, piano, and harmonica. Bluesmen couldn't afford to be picky. They played whatever they could find, y'know?"

It was apparent to Dee that Tooey was in no shape to help Clacker take on Salt, but at least he wasn't answering Salt's questions anymore.

Salt went on, "The children of slaves took the music they'd heard in their massa's churches, added jungle beats and the faraway voices that come out of those places from where their people, their souls, was stole from.

"Blues was raw, man, red-light. When the devil fell from heaven he pulled the Blues down with him. Put 'em in Pandora's Box and waited until he saw people still mistreating each other even after they knew better. Wasn't the devil's fault. It was man opened that box, let the Blues out. Man done it to himself."

There was an extended lull, a lingering silence. Dee fractured it with a whisper. "Clacker. What are we going to do?"

"I've told you. Break this window. Get somebody to call the cops."

"If your gun had fired you'd have had all the attention you could ask for."

"If my aunt had balls she'd be my uncle," Clacker replied.

"You can get us home," Dee purred. "I know you can do it, Clack."

"Give me a minute," said Clacker.

Dee justified her manipulating ways. She figured if a person finds a tool that works, who can blame them for employing it? That'd be like telling a carpenter not to use a saw.

"Heaven!" Salt snapped, then backed off. "Listen. I got all kinds of interesting stuff out here. I got a hammer. I'm going to break you like hard tack candy. There's a fireplace poker long enough and pointed enough to ram all the way down past your throat. I got a hairdryer I'm going to burn your tits off with, a bottle opener for your eyeballs, and a couple broken whiskey bottles. Guess where they go?

"I'm talking combustion, girl," Salt said. "Thunder. All the hurt you ever had up 'til now's going to feel like practice for the Olympics. Don't lack faith, Heaven; you are going to die horrible and over a long duration. Fun? Oh my Christ, it's going to be –"

"Shut up!" Clacker yelled. "Shut up! Shut the fuck up!"

Dee put her index finger to her lips and shushed Clacker. He shot her a screw-you-too glare before putting his head back down.

A puddle of tears formed in the corner of Dee's eye. She turned away, gripping the metal box ever tighter.

When Salt spoke again he said, "Nah, I'm just kidding. Let's make a deal. Open the door, hand over my case, and we'll call it a draw."

Chapter 41

Salt Wade was going to teach these kids a thing or two. He wanted to yell, kick the door in, raise the roof, but instead he kept in mind the young cop living next door. Salt knew he could wait out Heaven and her lackeys no matter how bad his ribs hurt.

He grabbed a footstool from among the scattering of heirloom relics in the attic hallway. Standing on the stool he could see just past the edge of the glassless transom window. He told Heaven and her puppets it was all over but the shouting.

Salt said he had a friend coming, a friend who would take the hinges off the door and help with some old tricks bootleggers used to use on rivals and revenuers. The choke pear was a good one, he said. Nice metal cone assembled in sections that spread out when cranked. Far as where insertion went, the pear was a versatile piece of equipment. Salt said he was sure his buddy had one of those with him.

"That ol' boy," he said of his imaginary accomplice, "gonna give you three the choke pear blues."

Stepping down to the floor, Salt wiped his knife dry on his crud-coated jumpsuit and poured a heap of white onto his blade. He blasted half up one nostril then the other, and realized pondering murder was harder than committing it had been. He could hear murmuring on the other side of the door, but neither of them said boo to him, and that irked Salt to no end. Set him to pacing.

"The harp," Salt said, driving a derailed train of thought, "shoulda' been more than it turned out to be, and nobody, nobody, played it like the Lobo."

"There was always fakers," he said. "Harp's small. Not a lot to learn. Even a half-assed player can counterfeit the moves without much sweat."

"But the Bluesmen, they knew there was much more to it than that. To play right, you gotta be ready to whip the devil's ass. There's a direct connection traveling from somewhere underground, up through the soles of the Bluesman's feet, through his body and into that harp. The masters flex and bend that sound with the skill of monsters. It is black magic, baby, in every sense of both words."

Salt sang the chorus of *Red Rooster*.

His throat constricted and his mouth went dry. Salt crept down to the third story bathroom and drank water from the faucet, splashed some on his face, wiped off with a semi-clean towel. He snorted another bump, ran water over his fingertip and inhaled that too. He went back and lay on the wooden floor that appeared to have never been swept. He could see someone lying down on the other side of the door.

"Soon as they could, a million black people moved north," Salt said. "In the South, if a white man slugged a nigger, that nigger couldn't do nothing. In Chicago, the Negro man could hit back."

He tapped a beat with his fingers. "The Blues is the music of slaves. Can you imagine? People treated worse'n animals. Slaves. In America. America.

"Jim Crow. Judge Lynch. Colored boys hung from trees for trying to go to school. Them girls in Birmingham. God Bless President Kennedy for saying 'no more'. Bless him. Bless his soul."

Salt took a deep breath because the whole topic saddened him. "And you pud-pullers don't even know what I'm talking about."

He got up, stood on the footrest, a preacher at his pulpit, and said as loud as he dared, "But you're damned sure going to understand when I get my hands on you."

Catching his breath, Salt brought the fervor of his sermon back down to a more professorial level. "Mississippi Delta's a pox-filled swamp dripping with ghosts. Plantations, levee camps, chain gangs. Mournful place. Choctaws call the Yazoo the River of Death. That's where me and the Blues come from—green hell. Where the white man's choir music got fucked by the work songs of his slaves.

"The Bluesmen wandered out of the swamp wearing harmonicas like beaver pelts. They was traveling snake charmers, spreading their devil-music scripture. People got infected. Wild-ass razorblade music. Wicked. Goes straight to the bone. Sparks rampage.

"We ain't the same color, me and the Lobo," Salt said, "but we share a lot." Salt had a finger's width of drugs left. He dumped some in the crook of his thumb and took it in with one healthy snort that made him shiver and choke.

"That voice of his. Man. Nothing but shattered glass and kerosene." Salt gagged. "The Lobo come up in them rotgut juke joints where the audience split their time between rutting like livestock and murdering one another. Long as they kept it 'mongst themselves though, didn't nobody Caucasian care one whit. And the musicians always kept playing right on through the fucking mayhem. But it gave those Bluesmen road knowledge. That's what I got. Road knowledge.

"I also got a can opener," he said. "I'm going to open your heads with it."

It was hogwash. He had nothing but his knife.

Salt experienced a sudden revelation, surprised he hadn't thought of it sooner. "You know the trick of the Blues? Don't make nothing better. Makes everything worse.

"Robert Johnson got poisoned. Sonny Boy robbed and murdered. Jaybird Coleman used to have to book his gigs through the local Klan. Think they paid that poor old boy right? Yeah, me neither.

"When Lobo was real little, his mama put him out for having the devil in him. Pitiful. Poor little fellow. Black as they come and not wanted by nobody.

"I'm getting riled," Salt said, and he was. "And that, you toothless turd, cannot end good for *you*." He stepped down, kicked the stool against the door, and took a hit of what paltry coke was left. It was dwindling much faster than Salt thought it should. Had he spilled some somewhere? In his pocket maybe? He checked, but no.

Calmer, Salt righted the stool and used it to steady himself as he got on one knee, whispering under the door. "The Blues is that raggedy ass little boy who ain't gonna be denied or ignored no longer, even if it kills him." He took a breath to make sure his heart hadn't stopped while he was on his roll. He put his knife on the stool. "No man can hurt you," he said, "while you're killing yourself."

Salt cleared a spot on the dirty floor and poured out the last of his coke. Lying on his side, he could see down the hallway. Under a knick-knack stand near the stairs was a surprise. The big stupid looking kid had dropped his worthless gun.

In the near distance, Salt heard an explosion. BOOM.

He said, "Hear that Heaven? Told you there'd be fire power."

Chapter 42

Clacker Herbertson had had enough. He'd had enough of Dee Bradnox, Tooey Walter, and the ranting lunatic outside the door, enough of the claustrophobic bake of that abandoned trash-dump refrigerator of a room. If Clacker had his way, right now there'd be a sea of police cars down below with lights flashing and occupants springing into action before their vehicles even stopped rolling. The cops would handcuff or mow down Dee's nut-job pimp or whoever this guy Salt was supposed to be, that'd be that, and to hell with the metal case no matter what it carried.

If he had it his way.

On the other hand, Clacker was never a quitter. You don't get to be your high school's all-star leading tackle through knowing how to surrender.

He told himself he should never have run away from this Salt character in the first place.

Clacker had tired of Salt's threats of torture and couldn't give two spits for those grizzled coons Salt thought were so important, but as Salt picked up steam, Clacker related to the anger he heard. He was letting Salt's fury seep into his own gut when the first BOOM and flash of the Fort McHenry Bicentennial midnight fireworks almost propelled

Clacker out of his ill-fitting skin. Tooey looked up dumbfounded. Dee trembled with aftershock.

Ten, fifteen minutes of rockets bursting in air, BOOMs Clacker anticipated yet still couldn't help being surprised by, BOOMs that seemed to interrupt every thought, and Clacker believed between the pyrotechnic bombardment and the room's stinking swelter he might go ape-shit bananas.

Clacker thought that if all he'd seen this weekend was what the world was changing into, he wasn't sure he could handle it. The Block alone had been enough to make Clacker wonder if life wasn't uglier than he was prepared to deal with. He'd never felt so full of sorrow.

Clacker glanced at Tooey sprawled on the floor and then stared at Dee. God, she used to be so gorgeous. She was still built like a— BOOM—like a soda bottle, but appeared much older than Clacker knew she was.

Dee looked at him with siren-red eyes. Clacker said, "I dropped the gun. Out there. In the hallway."

She shook her head, kind of chuckled. "Screw it," she said.

"Then I kicked it. By mistake."

"Didn't work anyway."

Clacker felt— BOOM—worse. He'd anticipated a barrage of insults.

"It was a Beretta." Clacker shook his head. "And I always liked that guy on TV, too. Tough, y'know, but fair. Got himself a bird." Dee was looking at him funny. He finished his thought. "But his guns ain't worth nothing."

Dee laughed until she cried. Her body shook with the sobbing. Tears left trails. "A city cop lives next door," she was able to get out. "Even with all that—BOOM—BOOM--that noise we could probably get his attention if he's home."

"Nah, let me pull Tooey together and we'll take this humpwad down."

⅄

"Tooey," Clacker spoke low, "Come on, man. Get your shit right. Sit up."

Clacker knew his ally was trying to do as he'd been ordered, but Tooey's body creaked with retirement home stiffness. Clacker pushed Tooey with his foot. Tooey scooted away from the door. Clacker noticed Tooey's jewelry. He added mood rings to the list of things that got on his nerves. Fireworks and the Blues had surged to the top of his inventory.

Salt was running his mouth again, but now with a shift in the way he sounded. Clacker listened and paid attention. "If you're thinking of sin," Salt said in a low rumble, taking extended pauses after each BOOM, "you're thinking about the Blues."

He said, "When somebody killed Sonny Boy Williamson with an ice pick, they stole his harps. Who steals a Bluesman's harmonicas? That's bad mojo no matter what you believe. Sonny Boy's last words were 'Lord have mercy'."

The fireworks ended with a grand finale and the world was extra quiet. No one spoke for the longest stretch. Years.

"Howlin' Lobo's music was the finest thing I ever heard," Salt said, breaking the spell. "First time I saw him was through a screen door. People fought to get inside, stole his harmonicas for souvenirs. The Lobo always kept two sets. The ones he played in public, and the special ones. The ones he used on certain records, the ones he bartered for down at the crossroads. They was Lobo's special weapons. He always kept them near, but nobody ever saw them.

"Later on," Salt said with an audible hitch, "The Lobo played through heart attacks, tuberculosis, kidney disease, brain tumors. All that. Played 'til the end. Lobo wasn't going nowhere 'til he was damned good and ready."

Clacker recognized what he heard in Salt's voice. Salt was weak, depressed. He'd gone from being madder than Mean Joe Green to falling apart. Falling apart just like everything else.

⅄

Clacker knelt next to Tooey. "We gotta get out of here, Too. You ready?"

Tooey eyes were clearer than they'd been. Maybe the rest had done him some good.

"Yeah, Clacker." Tooey stood. His legs moved like custard nailed to 2 x 4s.

"Get your wheels, now," Clacker said. "Take deep breaths. We won't go for it 'til you're ready."

"Ready for what again?" Tooey asked.

"You're going to snatch open that door in a minute and we're going to beat the life out of the guy on the other side. He's getting on my nerves. Can you help?"

"Yeah," Tooey said. "I noticed how he won't shush."

"We're going to stand on either side of that door," Clacker said, "and when you open it, I'm going to yoke him into this room and we're gonna put a hurting on him."

"Okay, just give me a sec." Tooey said, leaning back. Dee chewed a cuticle.

"No prob, Too. I'm ready when you're ready."

"It'll go better if you give me a second."

Before he allowed Tooey his breathing room, Clacker leaned in close and said, "I got something to tell you about Bradnox." When Clacker finished, he put his hand on Tooey's chest, pressing him to the wall, and said, "Hold right there until we say."

"Elvis Presley's' guitar killed the Blues," Salt said from beyond the door. "Harmonica never had no Elvis. Now every band has to have four, five guitars. Even the damned drummer plays guitar." He took a deep breath. "The harp's looked down on as a low instrument, like there's nothing left to contribute. But it's been everywhere, man, even outer space.

"Howlin' Lobo's playing came out of someplace deep and scary," Salt said. "The Lobo imposed himself on a world with no use for him.

"And he died at the goddamned VA, disconnected before the plug was even pulled. It was a full moon, and you'd better believe from heaven to hell there was howling going on that night. Ah-whoooooooooooooo!

"Yep, ol' Elvis did the Blues in," Salt concluded. "Rock and Roll. The next step in the devil's plan.

"And though I ain't got no onerous feelings against the Pelvis, I am damn sure gonna see all three y'all in the Judas Chair."

Clacker had come to understand that everything he believed was subject to challenge and change. Before this weekend, snakes, Charles Manson, and H. Rap Brown were all Clacker Herbertson had ever feared. He could take no more.

Clacker stepped to Dee. He said, "Salt's going to kill us if we don't fight. But I'm going to kill him first. You get out of here with Tooey quick as you can."

"I'm going to help you," Dee said.

"You run," Clacker said.

"You told Tooey not until he was ready." They looked over. Tooey was standing, facing the wall now; his head in the bend of his right arm.

Clacker turned and said, "Not until Tooey's ready."

But Clacker was lying.

Giving Tooey and Dee no time to comprehend what was happening; Clacker lurched, unlocked the deadbolt, and yanked the door open. Salt stood in the doorway, feral-eyed and with his arms down at his waist, his hunting knife on a footstool a reach away, Clacker's gun next to it. His face was red as war; his pupils surrounded by road maps. Clacker took a swing but missed, and Salt rushed him. They locked together. Clacker intensified his bear hug around Salt, and lifting him off the floor, danced in the direction of the dormer.

Clacker's last thought before he and Salt went crashing through the window was: "I'm glad Blue Lightning can't see this."

⚔

In the instant that Salt Wade heard the glass splinter, he looked at Heaven.

She was holding his case.

And giving him the finger.

It was a moment of clarity for him.

CHAPTER 43

Tooey was leaning headfirst into cracked plaster whitespace when Dee screamed his name. He spun and the door was open. Clacker clenched Salt so tight Tooey thought the older man's beet red face might rupture and peel back from his skull. Clacker and Salt tangoed toward the stained glass window, as if they were being vacuumed sideways.

Tooey attempted to hinder their trajectory, but his confused lunge was quixotic, his execution feeble. He landed with a thud where Clacker's feet left the ground. Clacker and Salt sailed away in a hail of fragmented colored glass.

Fresh air blew in, hot, but cooler than what it replaced.

The room decompressed.

Dee's caterpillar eyebrows danced from stunned comprehension to calculating. Tooey, shaking, stood. Dee took three outstretched steps and leaned over through the demolished frame of the dormer to scrutinize the scene below. She turned, shook her head at Tooey, and ran out of the room.

Adrenaline pumping as he dashed downstairs, Tooey saw Dee pause and then vault over Dr. Henry's body slumped on the second floor landing. There was less blood than Tooey thought there would have been, but when he tried to make the same hurdle, he slipped some on touchdown. He caught himself with one hand against the wall.

Tooey chased Dee out the back door. Midway along the alley, he reached out and wrapped a couple fingers around one of Dee's belt loops. It dragged her, earning him a dirty look, but she faced front without a word and regained speed. Tooey stumbled. Dee would let nothing get in their way.

A small crowd of neighbors gathered on the side street where Tooey and Dee emerged. Teenagers were pointing with enthusiasm in the direction of Henry Merriman's row house. A fat lady wearing a housecoat and slippers, her gargantuan boobs bulging out of a grandma bra, a pack of menthol cigarettes periscoping from her cleavage, watched with giddy dramatics as one of the teens mimed an exploding head.

Tooey and Dee walked away, fast, but not too fast. A few streets north they found a block of bars nearing closing time and they commandeered a cab. Tooey told the driver to take them to the Mohawk Motor Inn.

Holding the case against her chest, Dee leaned back, finally allowing herself to be out of breath. Her smile pissed Tooey off.

Three cop cars with their lights flashing and sirens blaring passed them going in the opposite direction. Tooey's head felt clearer than it had in hours.

The taxi pulled into the motel parking lot.

Tooey's truck wasn't there.

CHAPTER 44

Amy Ruari was exhausted. She'd worked overtime for a week, so she had an excellent excuse not to attend when her parents pressured her to join the family at the block party. Even her father relented, deciding to not force the issue. Amy couldn't imagine how her participation could improve any outing. She couldn't recall the last time she interacted with her family without bickering.

After work, Amy made cupcakes, and took her sister shopping. She fixed Carol Lynn's hair into a cute braided ponytail, and she slipped both Carol and their brother each a five dollar bill on their way out of the house.

Amy sat in the kitchen, pretending she lived there alone. She ate an apple. She took a long, cool shower, and dried in front of her oscillating fan with a fluffy towel. She slipped on a T-shirt she'd tie-dyed herself and pair of cutoff denims so worn they were more comfortable than underwear. She unwrapped the plastic from the latest cassette she'd bought, placed it in the tape player she got last Christmas, and sitting cross-legged on the floor smoked a roach she'd saved for the perfect opportunity.

Amy thought of Tooey. He was so bald-faced different from all the backward adolescents and cocky hoodlums she knew. This tanned, well-built fisherman, this Tooey, was nothing if not kissable. Which he was. Otherwise, why would she have kissed him? Amy was embarrassed by her own forwardness, but that wasn't the lone reason butterflies were flitting and flying around inside her belly.

She was worried Tooey had lied, that Dee was more than a friend. When first mentioning him, had there been something exceeding mere platonic affection in Dee's eyes?

Amy walked to her desk where there were sketches of a sculpture she'd been conceptualizing. What had at first seemed exciting and creative now felt childish, meaningless, a stack of kindergarten building blocks. She groaned and wondered if her lack of artistic verve was hampering her success in finding placement in an art school or vice-versa. Her bedroom walls weren't covered in teen idol or rock star posters, but were instead a gallery of her paintings: still lifes, portraits, and landscapes, oil and watercolor, some of which had won contests and awards. Amy liked a fraction of them.

Maybe she wasn't meant to be an artist.

Lionel Ritchie and the rest of the Commodores sounded syrupy, so she replaced them with Parliament's *Mothership Connection.* George Clinton. Bootsy Collins. Two of her heroes. Amy's father hated her favorite music. The two of them used to be so close, now all they did was disagree, so she worked at Polish Jack's while her dad owned a restaurant. The idea of her spending so much time down on East Baltimore was blowing her parents' minds, and the place *was* dreadful, but Amy always felt a connection to The Block through her magic Dahdoe, her father's father. Bernie the Bewilderer.

And now The Block had conjured her up a boy.

Amy fell asleep reminding herself that if Tooey ever did call, which was doubtful, let's be real, she'd have to remember to ask what the deal was with that name of his.

At 3:30 a.m. her private line princess phone startled her awake with such nuclear alarm Amy feared its screams would bring down not only her father's wrath, but the walls of her family's home as well.

CHAPTER 45

The buzz inside Tooey's brain, like a wasp trapped in a tin can, continued, but the soundtrack orchestrated by the insane had ceased. The needle had snapped, the tape was severed, or somebody murdered the deejay. Tooey couldn't say and didn't care. His head ached and his back was pitching a bitch. If he rested he might never be able to rise. But at least the din had died down.

"She's coming," he said to Dee, who sat on the curb, clutching the case and peering at the asphalt. "She'll be here soon as she can." Trying to evaluate other options, Tooey had resisted calling Amy as long as he could.

Now he couldn't wait to see her.

Dee raised her head and said, "I can't believe you lost your truck."

"Stolen," Tooey corrected her. "My truck's been stolen. Willy Nelson pulled a fuse or something so the engine wouldn't start and now he's stolen it and gone."

"The country guy?"

"Not the one you're thinking of."

"Still."

"You need to shut up, Dee." If she didn't Tooey was afraid he'd strike her.

Dee said, "You always had such a nice family."

Tooey knew it, knew she couldn't keep her mouth closed. "What?"

"You and your grandparents. I always envied your closeness with them."

"Yeah, well, thanks. How about we don't say nothing until Amy gets here?"

"Ooohh," Dee jeered. "The way you say 'Amy'."

Tooey walked away from her, but not far. She spoke louder.

"I remember seeing your grandparents," Dee said. "School plays, May Day, all that stuff. They were so sweet. I used to wish my parents were like them. Old and sweet and caring. First, second grade, I used to imagine we were married because then your family'd be my family too."

"When I'd get in tussles as a kid,' Tooey countered, "My grandfather wouldn't break it up until I got on top. He'd rather I take the licks than somebody think he was partial. My grandmother used to literally kick me in the ass. I wouldn't listen, she would not hesitate to park a boot. My mother ran off. My father died with a finger in his nose. That's how I grew up. Believe me, being a Walter ain't nothing like what life must have been being a damned Bradnox."

"You've got that right," Dee said, and sat quiet long enough for Tooey to think she'd been muzzled. He walked back to her. "And then," she said, "there was that other time."

"I'm telling you, Dee, you have to stop. Amy's coming to get us to take us home. Us and that case and whatever's in it. I'm going to deliver you to your father where you and him can straighten out what's between you. I never want to see you again, and if you keep pushing me I'm going to hurt your feelings." He pointed his finger in her face and said, "Now shut up."

"You think you can hurt my feelings?" Dee said. "After all I've been through?"

"You did it to yourself," he said.

"You would think," she said.

"Nobody feels sorry for you, Dee. I've known you my whole life and whatever goodness you had went 'pfft' by the time we were teenagers. You're spoiled rotten and think everything is always and in all ways about you. Well, it's not. Never was. And now you're used and desperate at twenty."

She regarded him with distaste, saying, "I used to think you were the hero, Tooey. All righteous and strong, quiet, guided by something other people didn't have. Now I see you're just an asshole like the rest of us. Yech," she said. "Some hero."

Tooey boiled. "You've been spoiled so stupid, you don't even know how far from a hero I am. I don't even know why your father asked me to come get you."

"Me neither," she said. "Salt handed your ass a concussion off the get-go, and you really, really helped Clacker back there when you fell down."

"I lunged." Tooey hung his head. "It's not my fault." Had his attempt to assist Clacker with Salt been half-hearted, less than it could have been? Tooey was too mad at Dee to think. He took a deep breath and rubbed his eyes. Then she did the worst thing she could have done, she turned on that throaty sex-kitten delivery and tried to use it against him.

"Oh, I'm sorry," she said. "I guess I'm questioning your manhood. Maybe because you always would rather watch than get in on the action."

Dee flashed her most sarcastic and wicked grin.

Tooey gritted his teeth. "You sure they were both dead?"

It took her so long to answer, Tooey thought she might not. "Sure looked like it," she said. She wasn't smiling now.

"Clacker had you pegged," Tooey blew up. "It's all yours, Dee, all your fault. You cost three men their lives because you're a petty little disaster who doesn't care who pays or who gets hurt or even who dies.

You've wasted everything you've ever been given and you're the most manipulative, ungrateful person I've ever known. You got the morals and self-control of a shithouse rat. You got no conscience. I wouldn't have you in my family."

"Fuck you, Tooey. You don't think I'm ashamed of what's happened?"

"Not enough," Tooey said, "and it's too late anyway. The worst thing about you is you're so stubborn, you won't even do the right thing when you know what it is." He wanted to make her cry. "Guess that's how you ended up a whore."

If Tooey's last remark landed and stung, Dee refused him any satisfaction. "Do you remember that night at the drive-in movies?" she asked.

"Yes," Tooey muttered. "Yes, of course."

"Tenth grade," Dee said. "I was in the back of Odie Adam's pickup parked along the far back corner. At first I was having fun. Kissing those guys, teasing them, and they started getting rough. I never knew where you came from, but when you yelled at them to get off me and they did, I was never so relieved. I thought I wanted to fuck them all at first, but it got scary and you saved me from them. From myself."

"I just happened to be walking by," Tooey said.

"Come on, Peeping Tooey. I know what was up. What'd you do, watch us pull back there and thought you'd come sneak a peek for yourself? See what was going on, maybe get yourself a little action too?"

"It wasn't like that."

"I'm sure it wasn't, Tooey. I've met a lot of guys like you since. You were going to watch, weren't you? Maybe get in a tug before going back to sit with your Mom-Mom and Pop-Pop and watch the rest of the movie? That's nasty, Tooey, but it's what turns a voyeur on. If I'd realized you were just a spectator, I wouldn't have wasted those next few weeks hitting on you so hard every chance. My hero and all, right? Turns out you weren't resisting my attempts to fuck you, you just didn't have the balls to see it through, did you? Not able to pull the trigger when the opportunity presented itself?

"I'd have made a little man out of you," she said.

"You are so full of it," said Tooey, stuffing his hands in his pockets.

"Did you know my daddy made me get an abortion? I was fourteen," Dee said. "First time I ever had sex, I got pregnant."

If this was true, it was new information to Tooey.

"Guthrey Kane did it."

Tooey had never liked that guy. "He's ten years older than us."

"He should have been put in jail," said Dee. "But I wanted it. I initiated it and I knew what I was doing."

"Except for the pregnant part."

"My father wouldn't even look at me. My mom blocked everything out. I was fourteen and scared. Nobody would talk to me. I wanted so bad to have someone good, sturdy, in my life like you, like your grandparents."

"Everybody has their own junk to deal with," Tooey said. "If you hate it so much, why do you want to go back there so bad? Why can't you just take a hint and stay away?"

Dee said, "I've got something to tell you: I asked for you to come get me. I don't know what my father said, but it was me. I asked him to send you."

Tooey stared at Dee and could have killed her. "You got me into this?"

"And you've turned out to be a complete asshole and fuck-up," she said. "I have something else I have to tell you. A couple something-elses."

Half an hour later, Amy pulled curbside in her battered-bumblebee jalopy.

"Do me a favor and keep your bullshit to yourself," Tooey told Dee as he opened the passenger side door. "If you never say another word to me in life, that'd be okay too."

Dee said, "And you know you did hurt my feelings last night with that crack about my hat, right?"

CHAPTER 46

Tooey thought Amy Ruari was the most alluring girl he ever saw. She smiled the smile meant for him. She wore sandals, cutoffs, and a loose ivory blouse with colorful stitched flowers at the open collar. He could tell she wore no bra.

He was still as infuriated as he'd ever been, but Amy's proximity cooled Tooey's revved-up emotional mechanics. He thanked her several times for coming to get them. Dee thanked her once, with limited conviction.

Amy navigated the pre-dawn city streets with proficiency. Little was said. The unease was oppressive. She turned her radio on, but religious broadcasting and talk shows were all that could be tuned in. One station, a preacher was barking salvation on this Independence Day morning while on the next, Bob of Bowie babbled politics. Tooey clicked the radio off.

Amy's 8-track player possessed a temperamental work ethic. It didn't matter. All she had was some classic James Brown, and funk bands that Tooey had heard of, but never heard.

They rode in silence.

Dee sat in the back messing with the case, trying to figure out how it opened. Tooey said, "Let me see it."

The case was as heavy as it looked, like it held a million dollars. Dee had clicked open the gold plated bottom panel that covered a combination lock. Tooey futzed with the numbers on the metal rollers and the latch. He caught Amy watching him. She should have been keeping her eyes on the road.

And slow down a bit while she was at it, Tooey thought.

He could see Dee in the rearview mirror. She had reclined against the window, her legs across the seat, her eyes and mouth shut; her presence innocent. A fondness for her swept over Tooey. He chalked it up to what remained of his concussion.

⅄

The Eastern Shore fisherman with his unpredictable, endearing grin needed her, and Amy couldn't remember being happier.

Not much was spoken between the three of them. It was obvious that Tooey and Dee were angry and worn out, so Amy kept her lips zipped. She never mentioned his bandaged head, blood stained baseball cap, or even that atrocious shirt he had on.

Dee was sleepy-eyed and pouty in the rearview mirror.

Amy's grandfather used to talk of old souls. How a person can have a spirit that precedes its vessel, has been around a few times. Now that she'd met Tooey and Dee, Amy knew, in two different ways, what Dahdoe Bernie was referring to.

Tooey was cramped, his seat back as far as it would go, his legs stretched as far as he could manage. Amy wished he were more comfortable.

Most of the way, the two of them, Tooey and Dee, first one then the other, monkeyed with the theatrical-styled case with the rattlesnakes, wolves, and gold trim. Amy kept quiet, smiled at Tooey some, melted when he reciprocated. Tooey and Dee faded into sleep, Dee snuggling the case like a teddy bear. They were children. At one point, Tooey mumbled, "Keep her in the channel." Amy didn't know what those words meant, but that didn't stop them from giving her cheer.

As Amy neared the Eastern Shore terminus of the Bay Bridge, the sun rose blood orange red and as big as another world across the flat horizon. Painting itself in front of her very eyes, Amy had never seen anything as inspirational as that morning's daybreak.

She drove much farther than was necessary. Tooey awoke, realized they were two counties closer to the Atlantic Ocean than they should have been, yawned, and said that the truck stop at the next stoplight was looking "awful-awful good."

Tooey woke Dee. She agreed that breakfast sounded like an excellent idea.

Amy and Dee ate big, Tooey twice that. Scrambled eggs with cheese, crispy-fat bacon, ham with a ring of bone, home fries, and an endless supply of hot buttered toast. Amy drank orange juice, Dee chugged coffee. Tooey sucked down three large sodas and a glass of iced chocolate milk.

They sat in a booth, Dee on one side, Tooey and Amy on the other. Tooey finished his meal and leaned back. Amy reached down, grasped his hand. He smiled. She blushed. Dee rolled her eyes.

The waitress handed Tooey the check. He gave her a twenty, told her to keep the change, and stood. He said to the girls, "I'll be back. I need to give Moviestar a call."

Amy couldn't begin to guess which movie star Tooey might know. It must have showed. Dee said, "Moviestar's his grandfather. They're close"

Amy saw a chance to address her concerns. She said, "There's nothing between you two I should know about is there?"

Dee laughed. "Oh no, honey. I told you, Tooey's a friend. He's not much fun, not the most polished track on the album, but I'll give you, there's always been something," she nodded toward the phone booth, "about Tooey Walter. Just not for me."

"You like him." Amy could tell.

"I'd like to like him."

The waitress, with no apparent interest in this or any other conversation, topped off Dee's coffee. "But no," Dee said, "he's too good."

"Too good?"

"You know, kind, even-tempered, boring. Too…sensitive."

"That sounds nice to me," Amy said.

"He's not worth much," Dee teased, "except for lurking around, asking a bunch of stupid questions, smelling like fish."

Amy said, "I can deal with all that."

"Then you better get him while he's hot," Dee said.

Tooey walked back into the dining room, his face ashen. He looked at Amy and Dee and said, "My grandmother is in the hospital."

CHAPTER 47

On the way out of the restaurant, Tooey poured a pinch of salt into his palm and dumped it in his pocket. Might not bring any luck, but it couldn't hurt. He ached to be behind the wheel. Amy tossed him her keys without his asking. Later he'd learn she never let anybody drive her car.

It didn't take long to get to the hospital. Before Tooey leapt out at the front entrance, Amy squeezed his shoulder. The gesture was as comforting as any Tooey ever imagined.

Visiting hours were restricted. The thin-lipped fusspot at the desk did not look open to rule-bending. She glared at Tooey with aggressive suspicion. He went back outside and came in through the emergency room. There were a lot of people inside. Fourth of July morning and the place was full-up with the injured, the sick, and their supporters. Some folks looked like they'd been sitting there all night. A discharged patient opened the door to the hospital's inner corridors, and Tooey strolled through as though he were an invited guest. He found an elevator and hit the up button.

His grandfather, sounding so tired and so relieved when he answered the phone and Tooey said hi, had given Tooey the room number. Moviestar said he came home yesterday afternoon, he was sorry but he'd fixed the boat's sputtering engine, came home, and there was Tooey's grandmother lying prone and bleeding on the kitchen floor.

Moviestar said he never believed people fainted, never seen it, but damned if he didn't black out when he discovered Ruth. He came to, probably seconds later, and was frantic with the fear that his collapse had cost his wife precious time. The volunteer ambulance drivers, local boys, said those few lost moments probably wouldn't make much difference. The doctors were less committed to that notion and reminded Moviestar that every tick of the clock counted when a loved one was having a stroke.

Ruth had struck her head on the countertop's edge on her way down.

A year ago, she had suffered bouts of vertigo. Tests uncovered nothing doctors could put a finger on. Far as Tooey knew, his grandmother had never been in any real danger. The dizzy spells stopped, but whatever caused that first blip of concern must have retreated and hid, then came back yesterday and tried to kill her. Moviestar said Ruth's condition was stable. It wasn't yet determined what the outlook for her recovery was or how long or severely she might be incapacitated. Moviestar had never been comfortable with doctors, lawyers, or government workers, and Tooey worried neither of his grandparents would know the right questions to ask. He'd never entertained that specific dismay before. It stumped him.

His grandmother was zonked with medication. She looked frail and helpless in her hospital bed. Beeping, whooshing equipment kept her alive. The tiled walls and floor were the institutional green and grays of bread mold. The room smelled sterilized. The atmosphere robbed a person of identity. They were just a human being on the thin ice between life and death.

But Tooey knew his grandmother was much more than that.

This woman raised two sons and lost both. She cared for a sad little boy carrying the weight of vanished parents. She was always shy, never the dreamy romantic. Dreamy romance was in her husband's wheel-house. Ruth's job was to keep everybody grounded. She acted like she had no patience for Moviestar's moony soft-soap ways, but it always flattered her and everybody knew it.

Tooey's grandmother had cultivated a crusty demeanor belying her mushy caramel center. Marching bands made her cry, as did Popeye eating his spinach, because it was in those moments Ruth felt everything would turn out okay in the end. If Tooey razzed her, she'd shush him and lightly smack his fingers.

Her smile, the warmest on earth, shared space with age spots, laugh lines, and crow's feet. At least it had the last time Tooey saw her without all the breathing apparatus.

Ruth Walter cooked like the blue ribbon winner she was, kept their home nice and neat, and was an active member of the Methodist Church and the fire department's ladies auxiliary. She loved to play cards and go soft crabbing. If pressed, she might have admitted her husband wasn't too shabby a man to spend a lifetime with.

Tooey felt as though he was writing his grandmother's obituary.

His stomach churned.

A nurse in white walked up behind and whispered, "You must be the grandson."

"Yes, ma'am. Is she going to be alright?"

"She got here in time and her doctors have been very attentive. She's strong for a lady her age." The nurse put her hand on Tooey's forearm. "Hopefully we can get her home in a few days. She worries for you and your grandfather. You're likely going to need to provide her significant care."

As the nurse spun him toward the door, she said, "You have to go. We'll both be in trouble if anyone catches you. Visiting hours are from one to three and seven to nine. I'll tell her you were here but that I made you leave."

Tooey tossed his mood ring in the hallway trashcan as he walked past. He kept the watch so he'd know for sure when he could return. The watch's face was funeral black.

Chapter 48

Dee said, "They're not home." Tooey wanted to tell her to get out of the car and wait, but before he grabbed the opportunity she said, "Can we go down to the beach?"

"You're home," Tooey said. "Tell your dad I'll see him when I see him."

Dee said, "Come on, Tooey, I've been thinking about Knuckle Cove. I want to check it out, remind myself of what things used to be like when we were kids." He weakened. She clinched her request by saying, "We'll show Amy."

Tooey knew the small and hidden inlet well. Knuckle Cove was where younger kids swam in summer and a make-out spot where highschoolers honored senior hook day. Tooey relaxed and pointed back out Bloody Point's long drive with resignation. Amy put the Gremlin in D and made a U-turn.

They traveled half a mile south. Tooey directed Amy down a rutted, overgrown dirt lane. He wasn't sure her car would make it. The trail ended at a long abandoned boat landing, with a path through the marsh and a slope to the Chesapeake Bay. If the tide was right, and it was that late morning, there would be a decent spread of sand veiled on three sides by head-high cattails and reeds.

The cove seemed even smaller to Tooey than it used to.

Amy killed the engine. Dee got out without a word and walked off on her own. She left the case on the back seat.

Tooey and Amy sat on the hood of her car and looked out across the bay.

"I'm sad for her," Amy said. "But I'm happy your grandmother's going to be okay." She patted Tooey's hand. A breeze blew in and cut the rising humidity.

"Thanks," Tooey said. "I'm glad you're here. Thank you again for coming to get us." He put his hand on Amy's bare leg. They couldn't stop touching each other.

"I'll be in trouble when I get home," Amy said. "I should call my parents, but they might think I got called into work. Everybody was sound asleep when I left. Maybe," said Amy, "I should take my chances and not call."

"You should call," Tooey said. "If you want, after we take Dee home, you can call from my house."

"Sounds good. Is she going to be okay you think?"

"People like Dee are always okay. The world's her—"

"Oh," Amy cut in, "I hope you're going to say oyster." Tooey wasn't sure if she was messing with him or not.

He said, "I don't think Dee's ever known anybody she couldn't wrap around her finger." Giving it a few moments thought Tooey added, "If she and her father could be straight with each other, they'd realize how much alike they are. It'd be dangerous for the rest of us, but those two together..."

"A lot going on there."

"You don't know the half of it."

"You never know," said Amy, "what burden somebody's carrying."

After a prolonged silence, Amy looked like she remembered something. She said, "There was another guy looking for Dee. A big sweaty toothless kid."

"He found her," Tooey said. It hurt to think of Clacker.

Amy lay back on the car's hood and closed her eyes. She bent her arm over her pink forehead. "Tell me about yourself," she said.

"Like what?" No one had ever asked that of Tooey before.

"I dunno," Amy said, "like show and tell. Tell me what you love."

That was easy. "My grandmother's cooking." Tooey spread his arms out in front of him like he was presenting Moses' tablets on Broadway. "This. The water."

Amy rolled on her side and rested her head on one elbow. Her other arm stretched out down her body and ended with long fingers resting on the pearly skin of her legs. Her freckles were a galaxy of promises.

"What are you afraid of?" she asked.

"Carnival workers," said Tooey, "and those baboons with the big red asses."

She giggled. "Anything else?"

"Embarrassing myself in front of you."

"How could you do that?"

"I don't know. The way I talk. I stammer when I'm uncomfortable."

"I haven't noticed once. I must make you comfortable."

Man, her smile said it all.

"What about you?" Tooey turned the tables.

"What?" She mocked angelic surprise.

"Now," he said, "you have to show and tell."

"I like deli sandwiches and sauerbraten. Root beer floats and T.J. Swann wine. I don't like beer, seafood, or anything served at Polish Jack's." Amy's voice was soothing, her accent still foreign.

Tooey said, "Ohhh, deep dark secrets."

"Thought it was a good way to sneak in that I don't eat seafood." She touched his wrist. The contact tingled. "I'll admit it's no swollen-butt monkey, but it's the best I've got."

"I want way more than that. What embarrasses you?"

"Uh, my favorite movie is *The Way We Were?*"

"Shameful. Come on."

Amy swatted at Tooey and he laughed. She laughed and snorted, which made him laugh more, which made her laugh and snort louder and harder. "So there's that," she said with her hand over her mouth. "And I have big feet."

Tooey thought her feet were faultless, and he wasn't even all that much on feet. "My toes are webbed," he admitted.

"What?"

"I've got webbed feet. My grandfather does, too."

She got to laughing and snorting and she sat right up. "Oh you have to let me see that." She reached for his Hush Puppies.

"No way." Fighting her off, chuckling, Tooey grabbed both Amy's wrists. She put her face to his. Her breath smelled of cinnamon fireballs. Tooey kissed her.

⅄

Amy grabbed the folded cover from her Gremlin's back seat, a thin, psychedelic pop art quilt, and she draped it over Tooey's shoulder. They walked shoeless to the beach, teasing each other. With her long, buoyant strides, Amy appeared to be traipsing on air. Maybe it was because Tooey was so sapped. Maybe it was just the last gasps of his concussion.

Maybe she really was.

Chapter 49

Barefoot, Dee followed the boggy path along the bay.

Dee never saw any value to living on the water. She understood people's romanticizing the region and how that translated into dollars, but for her, the Chesapeake could be pretty, and it could be fun, but it could also be mean and it almost always stunk. Dried up seaweed washed ashore, dead fish, all kinds of shit. And in the spring and summer, as if the marsh stench wasn't bad enough, when the piles of shucked oyster shells started stinking things up, it smelled like, well, she guessed it smelled like home.

Ah, she thought, home.

Dee liked seeing Tooey and Amy together. They fit. Amy was a nice girl, lovable and attractive enough if you coveted that land-of-fairy kind of thing she had going for her.

Dee wondered if her own parents had ever been simpleminded romantics like those two. The prospect was impossible for Dee to imagine. Until she rebelled, her mother and father had lavished and heaped all their emotional energies onto their daughter. A competition. Dee felt bad knowing her mother never stood a chance. She was daddy's girl hell or high water.

Her father would come through again. Dee was certain.

He almost always did.

And this time, this time he might try to understand, not be so mad.

He'd fix things. He still had it in him if he wanted it bad enough.

Daddy would find a way to get whatever it was out of that damned case.

Then he would forgive her trespasses as she'd forgive his.

Dee approached unprepared. She thought what she was seeking was further away, an illusion she realized was heightened by the extinct perspectives of childhood. Hiking along, Dee looked up, and there it was. She burst out crying.

CHAPTER 50

Tooey and Amy sat on a large, sturdy piece of driftwood that was once a tree limb massive enough for a row of tire swings. A mile off shore they could see the tilted tower of the Bloody Point Bar Lighthouse.

Dee was nowhere in sight.

Tooey loved the view.

"It's glorious," said Amy, looking out at the vista spread out before them. "Why in the world would they call a place this peaceful Bloody Point?"

"Some people say Indians massacred settlers here. Some say it was the other way around." Tooey pointed to a spit of wetlands jutting out into the water. "I've heard that colonists put a captured pirate's head on a stake out there as a warning. I've also heard stories about old-time skipjack captains shanghaiing sailors in Baltimore at the start of oyster season, and then drowning them at Bloody Point instead of freeing them and splitting the profits like they promised. The deepest part of the whole bay is right off here."

"Is that what you did to me?" Amy asked. "Did you shanghai me?"

"Ha!" Tooey laughed loud. "I think we've both been shanghaied."

They sat quiet. Amy picked up a piece of shell, examining it like a tiny sculpture. "There were Indians here?" she asked.

"Algonquin, I think."

"My family went to Chincoteague once. Are there places around here with Indian names?"

"A few, but that's all down the Shore more," Tooey said. "The Mid-Shore's old English. Old with a 'ye olde' E. This part of the world is named Queen Anne's, Kent, Talbot, and Caroline. It don't get more English, less Indian, that that."

"You're right," Amy said. "Sounds like white bread and mayonnaise."

"Is that what English people eat?" Tooey had no idea.

"You might not have noticed, but I've got a lot of Irish in me," Amy said. "I'm supposed to hate the English, whatever it is they eat."

"Then white bread and mayo it is." They smiled at each other, kissed again. Tooey wasn't sure what to do with his hands.

Amy disconnected. "Why's your name Tooey?"

"It's Wesley Walter the second. They used to call me WW. Two sometimes. It became Two-ey, but if you write that, everybody calls you Twhooey. So it's Tooey."

"Then Tooey it is. Tooey Walter. Not Walters."

"My grandmother calls us the singulars and that other branch the plurals."

"Where are your parents?"

"My mom left when I was a kid. My dad drank too much, especially after that. He was a late night…" Tooey remembered having to get out of bed to console his wailing, verging on suicidal father; it would take Tooey a long time to tell anyone that part, even Amy. "He died in an accident," Tooey said.

"Your grandparents?"

He answered without thought. "The best parents I could have ever had."

Amy slid off the driftwood and spread the quilt out around her. She sat cross-legged near the middle and offered Tooey the position alongside her.

"Is it nice to live here?" she asked after he took his place. "It looks like heaven."

"It could be," he said. "I don't know. I go from my grandparent's house, to the boat, to the bar. Most the time, that's my life – home, work, drink beer, go back home."

"If you're not happy," she said, "if you don't like things, change them."

"I think I already have."

Amy straddled him and pulled his shirt off over his head. She pressed into him. He felt her against his chest, her loose blouse between her skin and his. Their kisses were wet. Whenever he grew overzealous, Amy backed off a bit, slowed him down.

Tooey nibbled Amy's ear lobe, buried into her neck. The muscles there tensed. She arched her back. Goosebumps rose on her arms and wispy hairs stood electrified and straight. She put her hand to the back of his head, brought him to her lips again. He grasped her waist, her hips, and his hands traveled, under her top, brushing the sides of her breasts with his palms and her nipples with his fingertips. He pulled away and looked at Amy. Her face was flush and sporting a thin but impish smile. She opened her eyes to catch him staring, and her cheeks blushed deeper.

"So," Amy asked, "are you happy?"

"I am right now," Tooey answered.

⅄

It was swift, it was intense, and it was Tooey's first time.

They lay side by side a while, and were, for the most part, dressed. He'd pulled her close, with his arm around her back. One of her legs rested atop him, the other snug between his knees. They shared smiles, and light kisses, and little jokes, their playful conversations holding re-calibrated context. Lost in her features and in her luster, Tooey was someplace he'd never been. He hoped he would get forever to try and fathom all the enchantments and mysteries of his redheaded city girl. He was sure she would eventually have to show him pity and let him in on her secrets.

"Go get the case," Amy said, "I'm going to show you how to open it."

CHAPTER 51

The old forsaken Dutch Colonial was a shell of a structure, vacant for decades, with a lopsided frame, rusted roof, and warped, weathered siding. Even when Dee was a kid the floors had been dangerous in their frailty. The house always looked like a delicate gust of wind could bring the whole thing down, whether a pair of young girls were playing inside or not. She was shocked the house still stood at all.

Dee toyed with the silver bracelet her father gave her one Christmas when they both were still pretending it was all a phase she was going through. The bracelet's original charm was a horseshoe. To commemorate special occasions over the years, if they were on speaking terms, Dee's father would give her another good luck symbol for her bracelet. She had a four-leaf clover, a crescent moon, and a coral agate wrapped in copper. There was an entwined and tarnished II, the zodiac symbol for Gemini, with a tiny pearl between the twisted columns like the last grain at the waist of an hourglass.

Her sobs diminished as she contemplated the decrepit building where for two summers, the two summers before everything changed, she and her best friend, her only childhood friend, spent at least some of almost every day.

Delores had clung to her parents as a toddler. In primary school she would whine and beg not to go to school. Then Delores met Peach Butler. Peach Butler was a bad egg and Delores adored her.

"Delores?" Peach said, "What are you a hundred? You should just be Dee."

It was Dee from that point on.

Peach said, "I'll steal my dad's cigarettes. We'll go down to the old house, have a smoke." A boy was on Peach's mind and she liked to mull things over with some tobacco and a friend. Peach brought out both the tomboy and the girlie-girl in Dee.

"Drink this," Peach said, handing Dee a pint of stolen knotty head gin. They drank the bottle dry, and between Knuckle Cove and home, must have fallen off their bicycles laughing twenty times. They never got caught, but they never recaptured such glee either.

Peach was the first person to notice Dee's new little bumps. They didn't stay that little that long though, and with the tits came the attention. Boys were rude and abusive, but they couldn't camouflage their moronic lust, the nitwit desire Dee saw in their eyes. Their adolescent cravings crippled them, rendered them beneath her effort.

The men that sized her up were something altogether different.

It wasn't all men, just enough of them to be able to pick a few out of every crowd. There was never anything overt, no flirting, no touching, but Dee knew, and she let the men see that she knew. Teachers, distant relatives, friends of the family, all were part of Dee's ongoing experiment to test the extremes of her blooming sexuality, to find her confidence in an ability to weaken and stupefy men by her mere physical presence.

For a long time she thought her powers made her special.

Guthrey Kane had been the first step in the next phase of her studies. Guthrey didn't take Dee's cherry, she threw it at him. Right there on the rotten floorboards of this shaky but stubborn pile of weather-beaten timber and amateur construction.

After the abortion, Dee's bold and frequent delinquency surpassed even her mentor's levels of misbehavior. Dee always got caught because she did not care. No punishment, no embarrassment, concerned her. Any time her father was yelling, the top of his head mushrooming and his eyes bugging out in anger, in those moments Dee knew she had her father's attention.

He'd even hit her once or twice.

The one action to give Dee pause was Sheriff Butler cutting ties between Dee and Peach. The sheriff banned his daughter from socializing with Dee, and even went so far as to make sure they shared no classes at school.

Peach didn't even try to defy her father's ruling.

Dee was hurt for a long time by the loss of Peach Butler.

She recovered by screwing Peach's longtime boyfriend as her last official act before quitting high school.

Dee wiped her damp nose on the back of her hand and considered for a moment the last charm her father had sent her. It was a wishing well, from when she turned eighteen, at the beginning of her groupie period. There was no card, no phone call, but at the time, the gift had felt like a miniature silver bridge between her and her dad.

There had been a boyfriend after that, the bassist in a band starting to garner music industry attention. They cut demos, and record label executives came to shows. The bassist was all Dee's, and for as high as he stayed most the time, he treated Dee nice and looked out for her. Sometimes the band opened for huge acts like the Rolling Stones and Peter Frampton. One night in Cleveland, Dee fucked the bassist over for the lead singer, who forgot about her before he even finished. Word got out, and the bassist, though he never said much, grew distant and inaccessible until a few months ago, at their show in Baltimore, where there were no tickets or backstage passes waiting for her.

No one on staff at the hotel would tell her which rooms the band members or their entourages were staying in. Dee found the group by herself. Security wouldn't let her by. She threw a fit in the hallway, and somebody called the cops who escorted her out into the street. With eighty dollars, a carry-on bag full of dirty clothes, and a mandate from her father to never call again, Dee headed straight to The Block.

Dee stood there in front of the derelict house at Knuckle Cove, hating her own self-pity. She knew her tears weren't for this run-down old home, or her lost childhood with Peach Butler, her virginity, or her daddy. She was crying thinking that when she had *her* child, *she* would try to teach him that it was okay to disappoint. If kids didn't know that, they might never get over it happening.

On her way back to the car, Dee noticed a horseshoe crab, beautiful in its prehistoric ugliness, washed ashore and on its back, marooned. She poked the thing with her toe. Dozens of segmented legs moved and then, except for the stray twitch, froze in unison. Dee picked the crab up by its long spiny tail, felt its muscles react, stiffen, and tossed the thing gently back into the bay.

CHAPTER 52

Tooey watched and listened.

Amy said, "My grandfather was a magician on The Block back in the old days. Before burlesque he worked in carnivals and in vaudeville, and he collected all kinds of vintage stage and magic stuff."

"Like what?" Tooey asked.

"Like stage props – you know, costumes and tricks and stuff."

"Can you do magic?" He meant real, Tony Blake or Houdini, magic.

Amy tucked her chin and raised one eyebrow in a mischievous pose. "I thought I just did," she said, turning her attention back to the case.

"But yeah," she said, "I can saw you in half."

"Long as you're able to put everything back where it goes," Tooey said.

Amy faked a wince. "Ohhh, see, that's something I can't guarantee." They knelt on the sand. "The point is," she said, "one of the things Dahdoe collected was trick locks."

Amy twisted the case in her hands, examining it, touching it, rubbing her hand over different parts of the structure and design. Her lip-biting intensity drew Tooey in.

Together Tooey and Amy studied the case's forest scenes. It crossed Tooey's mind that if Amy knew what she was looking for, good for her, because he sure didn't. The sky, the moon, the wolves howling at it, the rattlesnakes, none of it was telling Tooey anything. He could study it forever and never identify a clue.

"Those look like sixes and a seven to you?" Amy asked, pointing at the craters of the illustrated moon.

Damned if they didn't.

Amy flipped the case to its bottom panel and the combination wheel. Her first try was 6667, her second 7666, and bang, the combination lock slid out to reveal a shallow drawer holding two miniature, old-fashioned, and identical gold keys. Amy grinned.

"Want to open it?" she asked. Amy presented the case one-handed like a tray of food and the keys a cat toy. Tooey couldn't even figure out where the keys went, so he gave the troublesome box back to Amy along with his eagerness to be awed by her.

"Okay," she showed him, "one of these keys unlocks this plate." The keyhole was under the handle where it would typically be, but covered by a tiny gold curlicue that pivoted counterclockwise once unlocked. "Then one key goes in like this, it's a double lock I think and…there you go, and you push this way, and the second key goes in underneath, turn them both, no, hold on, let's try turning them one at a time and… bingo!"

Tooey heard the click and watched Amy's face light up in the same moment. His jaw went slack like canvas falling to the deck of a sailboat. Amy handed him the case.

He opened it so they could look inside together. When he saw what the case held, this treasure that had cost lives, that could have gotten him murdered as well, at first Tooey didn't bull's-eye comprehend what he was looking at. Then it dawned on him.

There was a waterside rustle. Tooey closed the case just as Dee emerged, wading along in the shallows and lazy-slapping at the reeds as she approached.

Chapter 53

Dee thought Tooey and Amy were guilty of something as soon as they looked at her. Dee recognized guilt when she saw it. They held Salt's case between them. Dee hoped they couldn't tell she'd been bawling.

Tooey stood and gave Amy a hand. It was sweet, and for a moment Dee begrudged the other girl her happiness. Tooey said, "You give us a minute, Amy?"

Amy said, "Sure," granting Dee and Tooey each a gracious nod. Carrying the case with her, Amy walked back toward where she parked her car.

"Hey," Tooey said to Dee as they watched Amy climb the small bluff. He wondered if Dee could tell he and Amy had made love.

"Hey," said Dee.

Tooey asked, "You freaking out about going home?"

"It'll be okay," Dee said. She stuck both hands in her back pockets, shuffled her feet in the sand. "I have to make it work. For me, my parents, everybody, it has to. I want a chance to get it together, to accomplish something. I can't live like this anymore."

"That's good," Tooey said. "Won't be easy."

"My dad will come through. He always has. I make him so mad, but he eventually always comes through. When he hears everything, he'll know what to do, he'll know how sorry I am, and he'll take me back."

Tooey still didn't think Dee understood. He said, "What about the rest?"

She said, "Daddy will find a way to get whatever it is out of the case."

"The case? The case?" Tooey was astounded. He threw his hands in the air and spun in a tight circle. "I'm talking about what the hell are we going to do, Dee, about this whole mess? People died because of this. Clacker died. Over this damned case, over you, over me. You can't just shrug that off can you?"

"Believe me, Tooey, I won't. But *you* have to," Dee said. "You have to separate yourself from what's happened. None of it's your fault. Don't let it eat at you. It'll destroy everything if you let it. And *we're* not going to do anything. You're going to take me home, go back to your grandparent's house, and probably marry your little girlfriend up there in her rattletrap car. That's it. That's all there is to it." Dee smiled and the child she once was made a brief appearance.

"Is that how you've managed, Dee? Acting like whatever consequences come out of your actions are just the way things are and you don't have any responsibility in the final tally? You know that's messed up, right?"

"I didn't say I don't feel responsibility," Dee said.

"You've got to be held accountable for once." Tooey said. "You act like feeling is punishment enough."

"Sometimes it is," said Dee.

"Not this time," Tooey said as he walked over to the driftwood tree limb. He sat, and staring out at the Chesapeake he said, "The way you see things aren't always how they are. Look at it from the viewpoint of the people you let down, the people you hurt."

"First of all," Dee said, never losing her cool, "you don't know anything about feeling the weight of responsibility. What have you ever been responsible for? You know, Tooey, everybody thinks you're an okay guy, but you slide off into jerk territory a lot." She sat down next to him. "And you're mean."

Tooey buried his webbed toes.

"Look," Dee continued, "I know I'm self-centered. It's one of my plentiful worst qualities. But these last few years, it's hardened in me like cement. I've tried to figure out how to deal with it, but I'm defenseless. And even though it's a miserable trait, my stubborn selfishness has helped me survive."

"Couldn't you have just been what you were supposed to be?" Tooey asked.

"I couldn't stand it," answered Dee.

They gazed across the water that had influenced their lives in every way. Tooey's back tightened, but he took a deep breath and his pain relaxed.

"And yes, Wesley Walter," Dee said, "I am hard-headed, but I'm also putty. How else could I end up bending over in front of strangers and making kissy faces at them between my legs?" She nudged him with her shoulder. "I get what I want even if it ruins everything. That's my strength, cutting off my nose."

"You don't… ruin everything," Tooey said.

Dee said, "I never had the chance not to."

"It's different now. You have to make things work somehow, otherwise…"

"I don't think I'm capable."

"You're capable of anything you set your mind to." Tooey took a deep breath and plowed ahead. "But, Dee, Clacker told me something I think you should know before we go back."

"I got you into this," Dee said. "And I'm sorry." Her eyes were welling. "I was hoping maybe you'd be my hero again, I guess."

"Some hero," said Tooey. "You picked the wrong dude, Miss Bradnox."

"I have a feeling you'll get your chance again someday."

"I'll pass," Tooey said with a slight headshake, "on that feeling of yours."

Tooey and Dee each sat lost in their thoughts for a few moments.

Tooey said, "About your dad."

⅄

On the way to the car, Dee said, "I hope you'll always be my friend, Tooey. I've never had many."

Tooey didn't know how to respond.

"Will you forget this mess?" Dee asked. "Put it out of your head as much as you can, and try to let your life be more than just this weekend?"

"I'll think about it," Tooey said. "You going to set things right?"

"I want to," Dee said. And not being able to help herself, added, "But I'm thinking maybe I hold off, until I'm in a situation where if I flake later, my dad, my parents, will have no choice but to help me take care of things." Tooey gave her an exasperated, unbelieving look. She realized how she had sounded because she tacked on, "But, no, things will be different this time. I'm sure."

Tooey said, "I'm taking you home right now no matter what."

"Let's go see my parents then," Dee said. "If my father's not there, I'll go in and wait." They crested the embankment. Amy sat on the hood of her car with the case. She stood as Tooey and Dee neared. Tooey walked to the case, and flipped the latch.

Dee walked over and looked in.

She saw twenty harmonicas secured in green felt lining. They all had the name Howlin' Lobo etched into their stainless steel cover plates. A rattlesnake tail and a pair of dice lay in a hollowed out compartment in the back corner.

Chapter 54

Annette White Bradnox waved goodbye to Marella, the lady who read her cards every Sunday after church. Marella responded with a toothy reassuring smile from the other side of her living room window. Annette sat in the driver's side of the red convertible and searched her purse before remembering she'd put the keys under her seat.

Marella's reading had been promising. Most times, the psychic doled out mild cautions of troubled times to come, counsels with ominous overtones that were never outright threatening, and never, ever specific. This time she told Annette life would turn around soon, that her cloudiest days were past.

Annette was driving up-county to visit Hazel Ricks. Friends since grade school, Annette enjoyed Hazel's company above any other. Hazel was the solitary person Annette ever cared to confide in. Despite Annette's family's prominence on the Shore—her father had been an influential shopkeeper, banker, and politician—she herself never craved front and center attention or a wide social circle. Most of her siblings inherited their forebear's genetic gift of gab and glad-handing. Annette was thankful she'd been spared.

Annette and Hazel were skipping all of the Fourth of July commotions, and were instead looking forward to spending the rest of the day by Hazel's pool, followed by a late dinner. Hazel's husband, Charles Grover, had taken their two adorable moppets to his native Boston to experience the Bicentennial in what Hazel said he insisted on calling "America's most historical city." Annette and Hazel always giggled together when Hazel imitated Charles Grover and his puffed-up but kindhearted overconfidence.

Her new car came with a fancy cassette player. Annette listened to Engelbert Humperdinck. He and Tom Jones were her favorites. Her husband wasn't into music, a little country and western once in a while. Annette didn't care for anything twangy. Anymore, she and Harris shared almost nothing.

In the beginning, Annette and Harris, despite their differences, got along well enough. Annette loved having a little girl to dress up. Harris loved showing off their darling jewel of a child. And while he could be brutish, Harris was always proud of his wife's good looks and carriage. No one, not even the mailman, ever caught Annette White Bradnox not at her most pulled together. Nor, for as long as Annette or Harris had maintained any say in the matter, would anybody see their daughter as less than flawless.

Annette was taller than her husband. It irked him and she knew it. Whenever Harris forced her to attend some social gathering he knew she'd abhor, Annette wore heels. As their relationship deteriorated, her shoes lifted her higher each year.

After her parents passed, Annette inherited money but didn't know how much. Harris took care of the finances. Being able to pursue her interests was all Annette cared about wealth. She prided herself on not being materialistic even though she had to confess her convertible was nice.

Engrossed in her genealogy research over the summer, Annette's lineage was on her mind. Worry for her daughter invaded Annette's consciousness no matter how busy she tried to stay. Perhaps Marella's reading was a hint she and Harris would soon hear good news from Delores. Otherwise, Annette could never figure out how to fix her daughter, so she had long ago stopped trying.

She'd given up on Harris, too. Those two, Harris and Delores, were so much alike, clever but impulsive, privileged yet always insecure, starved for attention. And they were both so bull-headed. To think that at one time Harris almost convinced Annette to allow their fourteen-year-old daughter to give birth. Annette had put her foot down, and Harris had made the appropriate arrangements.

Annette could never compete with Delores for Harris' affections; she knew that from the beginning. Their daughter was the sole person Harris ever loved more than himself. It was such a shame how things worked out between them.

Annette crossed the Chester River Bridge, and drove into the historic college town where her friend moved when she married Charles Grover. She'd driven forty minutes from Bloody Point.

To Annette White Bradnox it seemed a thousand miles.

CHAPTER 55

Off to the side at the VFW's Fourth of July celebration, Harris Bradnox was so busy keeping his mouth shut, for a time he wasn't aware of the perspiration trickling from his hairline. When he did notice, he obsessed on it to the point he found difficulty in trying to concentrate on what the asshole banker standing next to him was saying.

His loan holder, his so-called friend, was giving Harris some polite but arrogant drivel about how the hammer was coming down.

Harris resisted wiping his brow. He didn't want the banker to focus on the outward signs of his uncomfortable vulnerability even though it *was* a hundred sticky fricking degrees and everybody watching the Little Miss Chester River contest *except* the banker was wearing damp skin and armpit stains. Harris dared a dab with his handkerchief, and goddamned if the banker's eyes didn't glisten a bit and the corner of one side of his mouth turned up a trace.

"I can't hold the board off any longer," said the banker, talking low.

Harris was disgusted, but he also took a measured tone. He said, "I can't believe, as long as we've known each other..."

"It's not about that, Harris, and you know it. I've finagled you a lot of leeway but it's not like it used to be, bud. Times are tight. The recession hit right rough, and things are slowing down again. We have half a million dollars out on land for a couple years with no return, our guys get concerned. I've been telling you this for weeks, months. Do not act surprised when I say we have no time left."

"You know as well as me," Harris said while giving a nod and a wave to a farmer in the crowd who happened to catch his eye, "that all my properties are primed to move. I've got four more contracts that should be signed by the end of the month, and I'm getting ready to subdivide those creek-front lots that'll sell in no time. We're on the edge and ready to tip. That sewer comes in along the highway next year, this whole area's going to explode. We both know that."

"It hasn't been rapid enough," said the banker. "Look, the board meets Tuesday. You've got bank stock you can cash in for twenty, thirty thousand. If you can make sure there's fifty grand in your accounts on Tuesday morning, that'll slow the board down for a while. Is there any way you can do that, Harris?"

Harris wanted to vomit. Life, as he lived it, now depended on his daughter. His stomach ulcers were cauldrons of acid and pain cooking on a gas burner that had just been cranked a notch higher.

Harris hoped whatever it was Dee was bringing home, or Clacker Herbertson if it came to that, would be enough to save his ass for a few weeks. Cash would be outstanding, but if it were jewels, or stocks, or Montezuma's goddamn gold, anything to buy more time with his creditors, Harris would never ask whose it was or how Dee got her hands on it. He'd tolerate her until she started dicking up again, and then she'd have to hit the road and never come back. He'd have her arrested if necessary.

"Can you? Can you do that?" the banker asked again as everyone but Harris clapped for the pageant's runner-up, a scaled-down version of the banker's wife. "Hey," said the banker, "how about some applause for my little girl?"

"I'll see you before closing Monday," Harris said as he walked away, spitting out a corrosive "old buddy" he made sure the banker understood loud and clear.

At least with the banker, Harris didn't have to employ that conversational affectation he used with most locals. Walking the VFW grounds, playing the community-minded good ol' boy, it had to be "Hey y'all, how y'all doin'?" and "Well, ain't dat sumpin'?" Some of these people sounded like they'd never been taught ninth grade English and he was getting tired of the act he put on for them.

Trudging to his car, Harris would admit he'd been over-extended for too long. He'd snatched up as much dirt as he could over the last decade, certain no one would ever buy it cheaper. Now his creditors were breathing down his neck, threatening to take everything at the exact moment the market was fixing to erupt. And since Harris had been the only real game in town for a quick purchase of large parcels, there wasn't even a buyer who could take more than an acre or two off his hands.

Harris knew his problem was that he was right, but his timing was off. Didn't take a genius to figure out that sooner or later Eastern Shore real estate was bound to hit. The key was when.

All of Annette's money was gone.

There was nothing left but the land.

If his daughter didn't come through, Harris was well and truly fucked.

He hadn't spoken to his daughter in months. Other than a little cash or a gift here or there, he'd stuck to his guns about Dee's banishment.

Then, lunchtime last Wednesday, she'd called asking to come home.

Harris had heard Dee was on The Block, but he tried not to care. He'd entrusted her with his heart. She drained it. On his darkest nights, Harris wished his daughter had never been born.

He had to give Dee credit, though. Her timing turned out better than his own. She'd picked the precise right moment to offer repayment of part of the fortune she'd siphoned off over the years.

Harris left the VFW, and stopped at the Islander Lounge for a Calvert and Coke. Dark and on the brink of empty inside, the roadhouse had one built-in air conditioner that dripped and rattled in its frame, but wow, did that thing put out. The chill air was a relief.

Harris knew he was in life-changing trouble. His daughter, who'd cost him incalculable amounts of money, prestige, and heartache, was his last hope. He was at the end of a number of ropes. For a man who always needed to win, his current footing had his insides screeching mutiny.

Annette's car was gone when he came home. Harris went up to his office, which he would have done anyway. Mabel was asleep on the couch. After an agonizing bathroom stop, he shooed her fat ass over, and with his loafers still on, laid down next to the family dog. Harris had a headache, and thought maybe he'd try to take a nap.

Within half an hour, Harris Bradnox opened his eyes, and his daughter, along with Tooey Walter, was standing right there in front of him.

CHAPTER 56

Tooey could not accept that "Good job, son," was all Bradnox had to say.

"Mr. Bradnox," Tooey said, "this has been the worst thing that's ever happened to me in my life. You and your daughter almost got me killed this weekend, and other people did die. I came up here to your office because your daughter asked me to. If I had it my way, I'd never have to see either of you ever again long as I live. Y'all are poison."

"I would not argue with you there," Bradnox said, walking to his desk. "Let me write you a check."

Dee spoke up. She said, "Hi, Daddy."

"Hello, Delores, you got that money with you?"

"No charade," Dee said. "That's good, I guess. Lets me know where I stand right off the bat."

Dee walked to the couch, sat next to the dachshund, and scratched the dog's hip with a light touch. Mabel opened her rheumy eyes and looked up at Dee for a moment before readjusting her roundness, and settling in as if her old friend's caress might never stop.

Bradnox pulled out his leather-bound checkbook binder. He turned his attention back to Tooey. "How much I owe you? Two hundred?"

"Five." Tooey couldn't quite tell if Bradnox was trying to cheat him.

"Pay Tooey what you owe him," Dee said. "I can't believe you. Rich as you are and you still can't help—"

"Rich! Ha!" Her father had a pen in his hand and his arms circled his checkbook like a walled encampment. "Girl, you must be out of your mind. Who the hell's rich when they're being bled dry by their own family? I swear to Christ, you act and talk like you don't have a brain in your head."

Dee said, "Still an asshole."

"You got that right," Bradnox said, "but let me pay this young man and get him on his way. Then you and I'll have a chat about who's an asshole and why."

"I don't want any more of your money," Tooey said.

"Good," Bradnox said, throwing his pen down. "Then get out."

Bradnox didn't fool Tooey anymore. Bradnox played badass, but Tooey could see through it now, the macho posturing was inauthentic. A pampered actor playing a gangster tycoon, this guy was nothing but facade.

"Don't, Tooey," Dee said. "He should pay you what he owes you and more."

Tooey was done with the Bradnoxes. "Listen," he said, "it's too late to fix what you two've broken. Nobody cares if the pair of you fuss and fight forever between yourselves, but now you're costing other people everything, costing them their lives. Maybe you can make all that's been sacrificed to your hassle worth it, I doubt it, but you better try. Because if you don't find a way to hold together whatever you got left, there's going to be endless hell to pay.

"You're family," he said. "You're supposed to stick together."

Bradnox chortled. "Kid, you're so full of crap, you should be a politician." He turned back and glared, pointing at his daughter. "Now, this one here? This one could have been anything she wanted. She had all the gifts. All the opportunity."

"Love her then," Tooey said. "She's yours."

"Trouble with that is," said Bradnox, "my daughter's got no regard for love or money or anything else. All she's ever cared about is what she wants right this second. In the long run, Dee couldn't care less for anybody other than herself. She's a bulldozer."

Dee, her tone changed, said, "I'm ready to be better, Daddy, I want to be a good daughter, a good... I'm coming home, because it's time. I'm done living like I was. I can help you with the business. Mommy will start feeling better. She and I can do things together and that'll make her happy again. It's going to be okay. Just give me a chance."

"I've given you a million chances," Bradnox answered. "Have you got my money? The money you said you were going to bring to pay me back with? Do you have it?"

"No."

"Then both of you get out," Bradnox yelled, took a breath, and continued in a calmer manner. "Don't ever come here again, Dee. I'll have you locked up for good. Maybe put you in the nuthouse next time. See if that works."

Tooey could not understand what he was hearing. He was glued to his spot, feeling as though the tension would not allow him to move a muscle or put together a lucid thought. The dog sat up, whimpering.

Bradnox said, "Go home, Mabel."

Dee stood. Mabel jumped to the floor with studied caution. Before Dee opened the door, she crouched down, and gave the dog a scratch under the chin. Mabel looked at Harris Bradnox with reluctance, and waddled out the door.

From behind the desk, Bradnox started. "You have broken my heart for the last time. I told you I had written you off, was done with you, never wanted you back. You think I didn't mean that, Delores? You think your mother and I can take one more shot?"

"I don't know—"

"You're damned right you don't know. You don't know anything. You don't know the pain you have caused in our lives. You don't know the arguments we've had, the toll your behavior has taken on our relationship and our relationships with other people. The cost of the embarrassment—"

"You've only ever cared what other people think and how much things cost."

"You don't know anything."

"I know you don't love me," said Dee.

"Like I said, kid," Bradnox shook his head, "you just don't know."

"I don't know what?"

Bradnox softened. He said, "You don't know how much I love you." Tooey could now see the man was green around the gills. Beads of sweat streamed down the sides of his face. "You don't know I have damned sure sat right there," he pointed at the couch, "and cried. I have cried and I have prayed for you many, many times, Delores. If that's not what love is, I don't know anything."

"You were crying and praying for yourself," Dee said. "I hate braggarts and complainers, and you're both. If you loved me I wouldn't have to buy you back."

"We put all our hopes into you. You screwed us at every turn." Bradnox addressed Tooey. "She does that. She tortures the people she says she cares for. There's probably a lot about my sweet little girl you don't know. You know she used to have the hots for you? Talked about you constantly. What were you, Dee, fourteen, fifteen? Oh, yeah, infatuated. Then you know what she did last week? Turned around and sold you out. Put you in danger, boy. You know she's the one who got me to send you to the big city?"

"He knows, Daddy."

"Big boy find you?" Bradnox asked without specifying who should answer.

"Clacker's not coming home," Tooey said. He held Bradnox most responsible.

"So I can only guess," Bradnox said, "whatever happened to Herbertson is what's got you all worked up, son. Well, be glad it looks like all you got was banged around. Delores has a way of bringing destruction to everything that crosses her path. You better get on out of here before you get completely sucked into her whirlpool and drown."

Dee's voice was almost inaudible. "Did you tell Clacker to kill me and Tooey if he had to, Daddy?"

Bradnox considered his daughter's question. "I gave him permission to do whatever was necessary."

Except for a short-lived quiver of her bottom lip, Dee appeared unshaken.

"Necessary?" Tooey freaked. "How could killing your own daughter ever be necessary?"

"Boy," Bradnox said, "this one has bled me dry, I tell you. I'm done. I need back all the money she's blown. Every goddamn penny. I hate the sight of her. So yes, Herbertson had my permission to do whatever was necessary to get back what Delores owes me, what she promised to bring home as repayment for some of what she's cost me over the years."

"And me?" Tooey asked.

"Who gives a fuck about you?" Bradnox answered.

"I do, daddy. I give a fuck about him." Dee pulled Clacker's pistol from the waist of her jeans. She aimed it at her father with both hands. Bradnox rose from his chair. Tooey had forgotten about the handgun. He recoiled in surprise, and then began inching closer to Dee.

"Is this the gun you gave him Daddy?" She was shaking. "You gave a boy a gun and said go shoot my daughter?"

Bradnox said, "It wasn't like that, Dee."

"What was it like?" Dee wanted to know.

"It was like living hell," he said. "It has been for a long time, kiddo." Dee's father smiled at her. It looked genuine. Bradnox said, "You're pretty as ever."

"You let me down when it counted most, Daddy," Dee said. "All my scars are in your disappointments."

Tooey snatched the derringer from Dee's grasp. It was easy to do. She registered no reaction and her arms went limp. Tooey held the firearm alongside his leg, pointing the barrel at the ground. He said, "This is way out of hand. Dee, come with me. Let's go." Tooey turned and grabbed Dee by the forearm. He took a step toward the door. "When everybody calms down you can try again."

Dee stood her ground.

Tooey turned back around just as Harris Bradnox reached above his safe, pulled the showpiece 12-gauge shotgun from off the wall, and pointed it at his only child. "Everything I've done for you and you are going to point a gun at me?" he cried. "Your own father? The one person who has always loved you no matter what? Who would have given you anything? How sick are you?"

"I'm pregnant."

Dee's words staggered Bradnox. He said, "You're lying. You better be, because if you think you're going to come home and have some baby from who knows who under the safety of this household, you *are* ready for the nuthouse."

"I want to do right," Dee said.

"*If* you're pregnant," Bradnox said, "you might think so, but you'll take off, probably not too long after that bastard's born, and leave your mother and me to raise it, to clean up your mess as always, and we are not equipped to do that."

"At the very least," Dee said "my baby deserves a roof over its head. Maybe it'll grow into what you wanted me to be. I don't blame you for all that's happened, I blame myself. I love you, too, Daddy. Please don't hate me."

Bradnox hung his head, but did not lower his gun. "I could never hate you."

"I'm pregnant," Dee said again.

"Don't say that again," her father said.

"Look at me."

"I can't."

"Look at me."

"I can't."

"Daddy, I'm preg—"

Bradnox looked up. Tooey saw father and daughter's eyes lock in the heartbeat before Harris Bradnox pulled the trigger and shot Dee in her chest.

Everything in the room rattled. Bradnox looked at Tooey like it had slipped his mind the younger man was standing there. He pivoted toward Tooey, and Tooey saw the shotgun's double barrel swinging his way.

Chapter 57

Without thought or hesitation, Tooey lifted the pistol in his hand and aimed at the man pointing a hot shotgun at him. He said, "Don't do it, Mr. Bradnox."

"I already did," said Bradnox. His eyes filled. "The Herbertson boy's dead?"

"Yes, sir," Tooey said.

"Where'd your stutter go?" Bradnox asked.

"I don't know," Tooey said. "Guess I grew out of it."

Bradnox nodded at his daughter, supine and emptied of life on her father's office floor. "I could never get her to straighten up and fly right," Bradnox said.

"I know, sir," Tooey said.

"I loved her so much."

"I know, sir."

Tooey put subtle pressure on the trigger. He knew he did not want to die, but he also knew he didn't want to have to kill either.

He did *not* know if the weapon would fire if he decided he had to use it.

Bradnox flinched.

Tooey realized what was about to happen.

He shouted, "No, Mr. Bradnox, don't—!"

But he never got a chance to finish.

In one fluid action, Bradnox swung his gun heavenward, placed the barrel in his own mouth, and right there in front of Tooey, blew the top of his head across the ceiling.

Bradnox and his shotgun fell behind the desk and out of sight. The eventual settling of pictures on the wall brought a quiet Tooey had never heard before. A wisp of smoke curled up from where Bradnox had dropped, but then dissipated and was gone.

Tooey tried not to look at Dee. It was impossible. With trembling hands, he wiped the pistol off, and placed it on her father's desk. Next to the gun, he laid the photograph of Dee that Bradnox had given him three days before.

Tooey closed his eyes and stood stock still. He forced himself to breathe. In his mind he replayed the loss and violent frenzy of the past days, and he swore on Dee's warning he would try to make this the last time he'd allow such permeating grief and regret wash over him. His emotional pain began to recede. The tide of perception returned. He allowed nothing but the essential answers of who he was and what his life should be swim back in.

On his way out the door, Tooey decided how he would be paid.

⅄

"Cool guitar." Amy said from behind the wheel, the carrying case full of harmonicas next to her on the passenger seat. "We should start a band."

Tooey placed the guitar in the back seat. It would be years before he could bring himself to tell Amy what happened in Harris Bradnox's office that day. "Dee's father wanted me to have it."

"Must be a nice enough guy," Amy said.

"He's something." Tooey sat down with the case on his lap.

"Hear that thunder?" Amy asked. "It's been building for a while."

"Yeah," he said. "Sometimes those storms get pulled north up the bay and never hit. You can watch them go right on by."

Tooey wanted to tell Amy how much she already meant to him, but he had no words for that. He hoped he had a lifetime to learn a few.

Instead he said, "You want to go say hello to my grandfather?"

The Bay Weekly Observer
July 19, 1976

VIOLENT DEATHS ROCK COUNTY

Area residents remain stunned by the deaths of prominent local developer Harris Bradnox and his daughter Delores earlier this month. Though thorough and complete autopsy reports have not yet been filed, Maryland State Police and the sheriff's office confirm that no suspects are being sought in connection with the events that took place on Independence Day at the Bloody Point home of the deceased.

Investigators report that it is uncertain exactly how the deaths occurred, though it is believed an ongoing family dispute consummated in an altercation leading to the use of nearby firearms. The theory holding most credibility with authorities at this time is that Mr. Bradnox shot his daughter prior to committing suicide.

Mrs. Harris Bradnox, who has been hospitalized twice since the loss of her daughter and husband, has, with the encouragement of her doctors and law enforcement officials, been traveling out of state with a friend.

Blues News Magazine
July, 2010
News & Notes

Last month, on the 100th anniversary of Howlin' Lobo's birthday, the museum in his hometown of Eastpoint, Mississippi, received an anonymous package containing 20 of the legendary bluesman's hand engraved harmonicas believed to have been stolen after his death at an Illinois Veteran's Administration Hospital in 1976. The harmonicas were inside a specially made carrying case that only a few confidantes, including Howlin' Lobo's widow and select members of his band, were aware existed. The museum extends its gratitude for the return of these important artifacts of American culture and music.

The Baltimore News Sun
July 29, 1976

RATS EAT AMERICA'S BIRTHDAY CAKE

The 35-ton Bicentennial Birthday Cake that Baltimore politicians promoted as a secure economic investment, as well as an opportunity to attract much needed good publicity to the city, may end up costing tax payers as much as $70,000. City officials confirm that the project's significant financial deficit is the result of numerous factors, including a rainstorm that washed 3,000 lbs. of red, white, and blue icing into the Chesapeake Bay several days before the cake's unveiling, tepid sales during the nationally televised Independence Day celebration, and the eventual consumption of approximately 40,000 slices of cake by hungry waterfront rats.

About the Author

Brent Lewis is a native Eastern Shoreman. Both sides of his family have lived on the Shore for generations. Brent has worked as a residential real estate appraiser for over twenty-five years, but has also been employed in various Chesapeake Bay industries, including commercial seafood and bartending for tourists. From 2001-2014 he oversaw the Kent Island Heritage Society's oral history program.

Along with numerous newsletter, newspaper, and magazine articles, Brent has published two nonfiction books, *Remembering Kent Island: Stories from the Chesapeake* and *A History of The Kent Island Volunteer Fire Department*.

He has one wonderful wife, one amazing daughter, and a cat.

If you enjoyed *Bloody Point: 1976* please post a positive review on Amazon. Nothing helps promote your favorite authors as much as a 5-star review.

Follow Brent Lewis' blog at easternshorebrent.com

Contact Brent Lewis at whiterubberboot@gmail.com

Made in the USA
Middletown, DE
20 July 2015